Geoff Bates
as the origin
shared or reproduced without the prior permission of
the author, except where small excerpts are used as
part of any review or reference.

This is a work of fiction. Names of invented
characters in the book are the product of the author's
imagination. Any resemblance to actual persons,
living or dead, is entirely coincidental.

ISBN 978-1-9804876-7-8

Independently published via Forward Thinking
Developments

Cover from an original artwork by Geoff Bateson

Other works by the same author include:

Everything There Is

Five Men

It's Murder on the Eleven

Another Glorious Day

Made in Birmingham: The Tales

Made in Birmingham: The Poems

Fragments : Lives

Vancouver 2017

Some jottings and observations

I'm not sure why I am even in Vancouver. A holiday;
a retreat; a time to get my ideas together; a time to get
some fizz under this damn book.

Looking forward? Or going back to my roots; back to
my birth; back to where I was a small child:
remembrances of lost times and lost opportunities?
Seeking certainties by going backwards?

It's not on the same coast. It's not even in the same
country.

It's not New York, that's for certain.

Vancouver is modern, metropolitan, cosmopolitan but
it lacks the buzz, the rushed brashness of Brooklyn.
The traffic is sedate – you could say pedestrian, if
trying to be funny. Here, drivers slow down and let
you step out. Back home, there would be a blaring
horn and at least a fair go at taking your leg off.

My stuff went into storage, leaving me free to roam,
to recapture some sense of possibilities. I could go
anywhere, do anything. So why did I choose to come
back here to where everything started? Why go over
things again? Why not choose Toronto and my
university years? Why not stay in New York as

somewhere to give me stimulation and to hunker down for a few months of writing.

There is a novel to finish.

No, there is a novel to start.

Months might pass getting ideas into some sort of framework. Then at least an equal time bashing out the words, then another several months of restructuring, reshaping and rewriting. Then the tedious phase of editing, checking, amending until there is something that might be close to a final form. So, a year or eighteen months from now there might be some inkling of a novel. For now, though, there is just a ragbag of possibilities, an empty notebook and some jottings on my laptop.

Whatever. I am here in Vancouver, for better or worse.

I have sorted out a neat one-bedroom apartment. Near the water, near the sea wall, near shops; not too far from what looks like an interesting public library; a short boat-hop across to the city museum. Lots of light in the living room. Quiet neighbours (so far). Low rent but not sleazy. Just right.

I am on the top floor. That gives me a good view over the low-build family houses with just a glimpse of sea in the near distance. It will do nicely.

The whole floor is owned by the old guy I initially took to be some sort of agent but who turned out to be part-owner.

He gave me the history: His dad lived in Edmonton but had been persuaded to buy a plot, way in the past when Vancouver was being established, and put up this block. When he died the building was shared between two sons – this one, who has the upper two floors, and his brother who has the lower two and lives in Winnipeg.

The old guy lives in an apartment on the top floor. The one directly opposite me. I'm at the front of the building, he is at the back. I get the sea-view. There is something special about looking out of the window and seeing water. It's where we all came from. It draws us. So, for me, a sea-view always lifts the soul.

So why did the owner, who could have had the pick of any apartment, choose the one at the back, the one in the shade, the one with no water views? He would be looking down on the residents of a cluster of shabby old wooden heritage houses.

Maybe that was it. Maybe he saw himself as lord of a very small manor, looking down on others who owned property left over from the past whilst he looked out from his modern tower in the sky.

He certainly has that air about him.

*

I bumped into him as I was moving in. His apartment is opposite mine. Next to his, middle of three on the short corridor, belonged to a Raphael: '… but he just comes and goes as he pleases,' said with some feeling.

Beyond that, end apartment at the back: 'Korean couple. Nice enough, but gone home to see family for a few weeks. You might not even notice when they are back.'

'Opposite them, in the corner there, is Sam, the caretaker. Ask him if you need to know how anything works.'

The old guy went silent as he turned his focus, past the elevator, to the apartment next to mine.

'That was Elizabeth's room.'

That was all I got. I caught something in his breath as he turned away from me and into his own apartment. No explanation of who Elizabeth was or is.

A daughter? Dead? Abducted? Absconded? The room kept as it was the moment she left: A shrine to her memory ….?

The block is quiet enough. No comings; no goings. No distractions or diversions. I might even get some writing done. Deserted (Not me, the building –

although I do feel a bit bereft at the moment: a lack of ideas that have momentum; a loss of New York routines.) – A bit of the Marie Celeste about the place, except that that is a cliché and such things are to be avoided at all costs.

An hour later I found a note pushed under the door:

The cremation of Elizabeth will be tomorrow at 11.00. You didn't know her, but her presence still looms over this place. Come along if you want. I understand if you would prefer not to. A car will be leaving out front at 10.30 sharp. There is a space in it if you want it. Malcolm.

*

10.30 as promised. There were five others in the car: Malcolm; the coming and going Raphael; caretaker Sam; and a couple of old women who came over from the next street up. It seems that Elizabeth was a neighbour of theirs. Lived in one of the old timber houses behind the apartment block, directly below Malcolm's balcony. So he wouldn't be looking down on the neighbours, he would be looking out for Elizabeth. But, if she lived down on that street, why was the apartment next to mine 'Elizabeth's Room'?

And she was old – not his absconding daughter but someone older than him.

The chapel held a dozen people. Beyond us six, there was a scattering of people who could have been neighbours. They knew the other two women from the car.

There was a rather stiff-looking woman on the front row, alone.

The service was short: Abrupt might be the word; curt, even. It was over before it began. No stretched-out glorifying of the dead.

There was the briefest outline of Elizabeth's life. She was born in Poland; the family moved to Germany when she was a toddler, and on to the UK when she was a small child.

I guess that was all something to do with the outbreak of war; something around 1935-1945. A life set on a trajectory not of her choosing.

For some reason she ended up in Vancouver and was briefly part of an emerging art scene.

Elizabeth spent a time looking after her ill mother in the home she had grown up in.

There was no mention of any husband and a nod towards the woman in the front row as 'one daughter, Margaret'.

There seemed to be a tension in every brief sentence. Elizabeth and her mother; Elizabeth and her daughter; Elizabeth and life in general. Things were said as pleasantly as possible but with just a hint of harmonies and subtexts.

Things moved on quickly, with a hymn (chosen for no reason that was apparent), a prayer (that went over the heads of most present) and an invitation to 'spend a short time having refreshments and remembering Elizabeth' – even that sounded like an invitation to go away as soon as was respectable.

There were sandwiches and drinks at a nearby bar. Malcolm got involved in an awkward-looking conversation with the daughter. Raphael sulked most of the way through. Friends and neighbours chatted amongst themselves. I hung around, observing, looking for angles.

No-one stayed long. The daughter stalked out. The old neighbour-friends sat drinking and taking advantage of a free lunch before drifting off together. Sam went off by himself, saying he had stuff to buy. Malcolm checked if I was good for getting back on my own then he and Raphael went off, talking in a way that was both intimate and angry at the same time. I finished off a few more sandwiches then headed across to the SkyTrain.

The sense I was left with was that Elizabeth was isolated: Moved from place to place and ended up with no parents around, no children other than black-coated Margaret, no cousins or extended family (none that had come to see her off, anyway). No great social network, built up over years in Vancouver. She died alone.

Who were you, Elizabeth – really, deep down?

Malcolm said you were some sort of shadow lingering over his apartment block and that is how you seem: shadowy, insubstantial, ethereal. Who were you: beyond being a carer for an aged mother, a mother of a stiff-bodied daughter, a daughter of parents who took you across the globe?

Where is the You? Or is that all there is – mothers and daughters – caring and ceasing to care – a life of women's work until you died, remembered by a small handful of people?

And how did you die? Peacefully in that quaint bit of Vancouver heritage? Of some illness we weren't told about? An accident whilst doing something exciting?

And how would I want you to have died (if you are going to be some character in my writing)?

You died just over two weeks ago; just as I left New York. That was around the time of Trump's Inauguration. So, that could be one set of coincidences - correlations not causalities: Trump into office and I leave New York; Trump into office and Elizabeth dies; I leave New York and Elizabeth dies.

I imagine her, clinging to the remnants of a life, furious that all she had done, all she had worked for, all that being dragged from country to country, all her hopes and ambitions, had come to this – Trump as The Chief of the Free World. I see her apoplectic, raging and railing at the TV picture as he promises to be a good boy and do as expected. I imagine her collapsing as her heart breaks.

A life fleeing from things. A life taking care of things. A life of artistry and neighbourliness. All ending in disappointment. All ending in an overpowering sense of pain. Maybe there was one last attempt at resistance – throwing the book she had been reading, hitting him square on the jowl, but unable to stem the flow of words, unable to whack the look off his face.

I imagined her doing all that as she slid from the chair, crumpling in resignation and death.

*

I've seen the sun. I had forgotten that it rains so much in Vancouver – providing endless variations in conversation around horizontal rain, drenching rain, light rain that is probably going to clear later, and so on.

I went for a walk to the seafront. Even that involved a choice: right to Robson and Coal Harbour, or left to Davie and English Bay. I went right. It turned out to be the right choice. It took me to something quite magical: float planes all lined up. Occasionally one would taxi away from the landing stage, take a long arc to the end of the inlet, then clatter along the water, gaining speed, urging itself airborne, like some cranky goose; then banking away into the thin cloud at the head of the mountain. Transporting people. A modern-day mule; a mechanical packhorse. Human cargo shuttled into the city at the start of the day and shuttled back out at the end. What a way to commute – to sense the plane freeing from the drag of the water, soaring, lifting.

I turned right at the waterfront, towards the dock by the Conference Centre. A heavier transport towering against it: the tiered decks of a cruise ship. Here as one stop on its list, spilling out passengers to wander dazed, to shop for trinkets with the name Vancouver on, to take selfies: 'This is the ship in Vancouver; this is the ship in Honolulu; this is the ship somewhere else – don't remember where that was as I didn't buy a souvenir there.'

All part of attempts to construct and reconstruct themselves through self-shot memories. Me in Vancouver; me somewhere else.

It reminds me of a visit I made to MOMA back home. I could hardly see the paintings for knots of Japanese schoolgirls taking selfies. This is Me and that Van Gogh thing, Me and that Lichtenstein thing, Me and that Jackson Pollock dribbly thing, Me and those Warhol soup tin things ..... Works of art dragged into frame to momentarily prop up their sense of self.

Right again, up to the library: a terracotta spiralling slab of a building, looking like some scaled-up exercise from a beginners' pottery class: 'Flatten your clay, curl it in on itself, poke in some windows and a door and you have a book repository, a people's university, where a writer in residence advertises sessions, and readers take up daily residence if only for the toilets, the newspapers and the sense of having somewhere to go and something to do.'

Right again, back down the long stretch of Robson Street.

This was once Robson Strasse (according to my pocket guidebook), giving some linguistic link back to Elizabeth's Polish/ German/ British/ Canadian parents.

There are occasional traces of those who were here before. First Nations. Waymarked by the occasional plaque on the seawall and totems in the Convention Centre lobby.

Right, right, right, right – back to near where I started. Back to near home. Strange how soon I have come to think of the apartment here as home.

I stop off for a coffee in Starbucks - a sort of temporary, universal, all-purpose home for people like me. On the first morning anywhere, I can walk into a global coffee chain and speak the language, know the prices, not get any surprises.

There are probably more than fifty, more than a hundred, in Vancouver. Millions of coffees a day. Keeping the sewers flowing.

So, the trip out ended with Starbucks and coffee before going to my fourth-floor apartment, with its homely sea-view out front and its writing yet to be done.

*

I don't watch much news, but I get occasional yearnings for an update from the US. Every time I switch on, I get the Leader signing this, signing that, frowning a lot, not saying much.

OK: I didn't vote for the guy. I didn't even vote but I treasure democracy and so, to my mind, he is the legitimate leader. Someone to be given a chance, same as all the others have had to settle in. He said he would fix a lot of things that really need fixing.

There may or may not have been dirty tricks. There have certainly been shenanigans in the past and any recent ones are just more in keeping with today: emails, hackings, tweets. What do people expect: That there will be little vans still going around the streets with loudspeakers strapped to the roof, and brown envelopes stuffed with dollar bills being handed out in smoke-filled backrooms?

What stirred people to vote? Their lives are crap and he lay the blame for that with elites (political, journalistic, managerial, federal) who had let it be so. He spoke their language and fed their views. He resonated with them and they cheered him for it. He said a lot of rubbish and drew out visceral feelings in a whole set of voters. People liked him or loathed him.

The guy went on record as grabbing women whenever he felt like it. Women took to the street in force. Yet other women turned out to vote for him, against a woman candidate. It wasn't that she was a woman. It was that she was an academic, a politician, always in your face.

On the local news, things link up with what I see each day. One lead story has been about the growing numbers of homeless people in cities across North America; and a new, lethal, drug epidemic. One by one local politicians jumped in, promising to fix things. None sounded credible.

Could be something in there for my writing:

Regular Guy living Regular Life until his routine gets hit by an unexpected rock. His regular life disintegrates. He loses his job, loses his home, loses his family and ends up on the street. Tries to get back: fails to get back. Tries again: fails again. He gives up. Drugs take the edge off things, but others die around him. Tries to get off drugs: fails to get off drugs. That's a common enough description of the path walked by too many people today – so what's the story?

Maybe it's a crime mystery. The homeless drug-deaths are the setting, the symptoms, not the main story. The story is one of organised crime, of hard-pressed police officers, of a Mayor and Police Chief facing hard political realities, of a press wanting answers. Maybe there is a whiff of corruption somewhere; an officer being made some offer he can't refuse. Maybe there is a link to overseas investment in property as a way of money laundering the profits from the drug trade. Maybe …. Except that it's all been done before. Is there some new angle??

*

Rain today. Not horizontal; not vertical. Not drizzle; not drenching. Just regular sixty-degree wetness. I had just settled down for a morning of writing when there was a knock at the door. It was Malcolm, red-faced. He has one of those florid, scarlet/purple-veined noses but this was full-face exertion-red: Sixty percent of the way to a heart attack.

He beckoned me to follow him into the next-door apartment – Elizabeth's Room. How could I resist?

It wasn't what I had been expecting. Not that I had been expecting anything, but this was nothing like the nothing I hadn't been expecting.

It was an artist's studio. An easel; paint-spattered floor covering; and stacks of canvases – some facing outwards, some with their backs to the room. And there in the middle of it all was an ancient-looking trunk.

I waited for him to get his breath back. He had struggled the trunk from Elizabeth's house, round the corner, into the elevator and up into what he still referred to as Her Room.

Still a bit breathless from it all, he explained that there had been a reading of Elizabeth's will at her house earlier. Margaret, the frosty stiff daughter, had been left everything except the trunk, which had been left to him.

He wanted someone else present when he opened it.

There was a letter with it.

I thought he was going to cry as he handed me it.

Malcolm dear friend,

I doubt if I got chance to say goodbye. Death has this inconvenient habit of coming at the wrong time, catching us unprepared. This is my feeble attempt at saying that I appreciate all that you have done for me. We both know that you didn't have to do any of it and that everything was due to your innate kindness and generosity (to a fault, if I can be presumptuous now that you can't rebuke me for it, when it comes to young Raphael).

You knew me at my best and at my worst – but, still, there is much you didn't know. I have always appreciated that you didn't pry.

By now you will know that Margaret (the daughter we didn't speak too much about) has control of my lovely little house. Although she grew up there she has never had much feeling for the place. She never saw it as home. It was a place where I was and therefore a place she had to be from time to time. Now that I am no longer in it, I have no idea what she feels about the place, or what she feels about anything, really. Or even if she has any feelings about anything. She is free to do as she will.

Anything that is of value to me is either in my studio rooms or in the trunk that is my small bequest to you. The studio rooms can be cleared, and I trust you to think of me when you get that done. The trunk is not meant to be any sort of recompense for all the friendship you have given over the years. No price or reward can be put on that. Instead, I am selfishly putting yet another burden on you.

The trunk holds things that I have some particular attachment to. Margaret will no doubt simply dump the contents of the house as worthless junk, so I am safeguarding some small treasures and putting them outside her reach. This puts the onus on you, I am afraid. Knowing me as you do, you are at liberty to dispose of the trunk and its contents in any way you feel appropriate.

I shall neither know nor judge.

Love

Elizabeth

'I couldn't open her trunk,' he said. 'I need someone with me. Sam isn't the kind of person to do that. Neither is Raphael, to be honest. I wondered if you might …..'

His voice trailed off and he looked at me pleadingly. What could I say?

The trunk looked interesting. I'm not sure what Malcolm had worried he might find.

Another writing possibility there: Old man is left mystery trunk by lifelong friend. When he opens it there is a mummified baby wrapped in an ancient shawl? A treasure map and a scroll tied with a strand of silk? Bundles of love letters from a fiancée who went to fight on the Western Front in the First World War and didn't return?

As it turned out, Elizabeth's trunk was full of odds and ends. The ends of a life. It would all have meant something to her or she wouldn't have collected it as, in her words, bits of treasure to be put well out of the grasp of her rarely-spoken-of daughter.

Malcolm closed the lid without disturbing any of it.

'I can't touch it. It's all too personal; all too close to Elizabeth. I might be able to do that in a few days, but not yet. Just like I can't look at her paintings. It can all wait.'

He wandered off, leaving me to close the door and head back to my own place.

From her legacy letter to Malcolm, Elizabeth sounds a nice person.

She had started as a total unknown. Slowly, pieces are being revealed. Fragments, disconnected, but enough to start filling out an image of her.

She was old – maybe in her eighties – with a daughter called Margaret, who was maybe sixty or sixty-five. She was born in Poland. Her parents moved first to Germany then to the UK, both when Elizabeth was a young child. The family came to Canada and ended up, somehow, in Vancouver. She has known Malcolm for a while but not, I think, for her whole life.

For some reason he gave her use of one of his dozen or so apartments, not to live in but to use as rooms to do painting. They were close friends but highly unlikely that they were more than that. She ended her life with him as a key contact, certainly as her most trusted person. He was a Significant Other to her: More so than a handful of neighbours; probably even more than her daughter.

She had a gentle language, with strong opinions lurking in there somewhere. She accumulated a small collection of treasured items that didn't look much for a lifetime.

I'm sure she held back some secrets.

I have the urge to find out more about her. There are more fragments to uncover and more strands to tease out.

*

Now what is the guy up to?

The photos show empty spaces where he says there were the biggest support crowds ever. Ever. He thinks that repeating something twice makes it twice as likely to be true.

He appoints businessmen with no political record, sets his family members to be his inner guard, acts like the TV showman he is and fires his Attorney General for not backing his illegal actions.

Glad I'm not American.

*

Post Truth: It's not about falsifying or lying.

Lies imply that there is a Truth out there somewhere, just waiting to be uncovered.

It's not even about claiming something else as the truth.

If you no longer care whether there is a truth or not, you can say anything for effect and claim it has some substance.

Simply by claiming that everyone else is lying he radiates the idea that he is the sole truthsayer in the world. 'Trust Me', he says, without actually having to say it.

Others throw around statistics on this; statistics on that. Who votes on statistics?

People can present all the facts they want. In response you can simply make stuff up and say it boldly enough. Reality is boring. Made-up stuff is far more interesting, far more startling.

Facts don't matter. Feelings matter. Gut-wrenching feelings matter most. You can't fight emotions with statistics. You need to fire people up. Mobilising the anger of the crowd is the new politics. Stoke their feelings of impotence and revenge.

Better still, claim not to be a politician. Politicians lie, we all know that.

Send your feelings out via those trendings and tweetings, let it all go viral and see what happens. Push out lies, rumours – anything that makes a story. Then push out anything that stretches that story - or overturns it. What is true, factual, evidenced, gets second place to what grabs attention.

No need for any provenance; no need for editorial checks and balances. Things are complicated? Make it simple. Things don't add up? Throw more fuel on the fire.

It will get believed simply because it matches existing beliefs. It feels so true that it doesn't have to be true. People want their feelings validated because that is what sustains their sense of who they are.

It pays to be outrageous. Say the unsayable. Be a firebrand. Contradict; exaggerate; insult. Be the one and only authentic politician who comes along, telling it like it is.

This is the age of the bold. This is no time for humility. The winner takes the prize – walking off with it whether or not they actually, factually, won.

*

It seems that I am now being given responsibility for unpacking Elizabeth's little treasures. There has been an exchange of notes under doors. I'm not sure why Malcolm isn't up to face-to-face conversations about Elizabeth, her room and her trunk but he isn't, so notes slipped under doors it has been. I quite like that in a way. It all adds to the aura of mystery, of secrecy, of surreptitious comings-and-goings in the night – even if the exchange of notes was done mid-morning. Skulduggery: that is the word that was eluding me.

Donald,

This may seem an odd thing to ask. As you may have guessed, there was a very close personal bond between myself and Elizabeth. I haven't come to terms with her death.

I would drop into her studio room most mornings, to chat whilst she painted. Now I am at a bit of a loss. To be honest, I cannot face being in that room without her, knowing that our conversations have been cut short. They were never about anything world-shattering, but they contained so much humanity.

She was, to me at least, quite a unique person.

I can't go in the room and I certainly can't go unpacking things in her trunk of things so personal to her that she saw fit to put them beyond the clutches of Margaret who she rightly suspected of being someone for whom personal mementos are of no value and are to be disposed of simply as detritus that a life has accumulated.

I am building up to my request, which seems such a big thing to put upon you.

Can you take on the task of going through Elizabeth's paintings and chest-contents?

I think it needs someone who can be a bit detached. I would simply weep over each tiny item and not know what to do with any of it. It may turn out that Margaret is right, and everything simply needs to go into the garbage bins. It's just that I don't trust my own judgement on that any more than I trust hers.

Raphael would be useless and, in any case, is going away for a while. Sam is far too practical. If things can't be screwed together or plugged in he has no interest in them. That just leaves you.

I sense that you might be interested enough to want to treat it as an enjoyable exploration; removed enough to be able to bring a critical eye to it all; yet sensitive enough to want to make a good job of the task. If I am wrong, then forgive my even suggesting it.

I have left the key in Elizabeth's door. If you want to take on this request, even initially until I am able to take over, then take the key and let yourself in as much or as little as you want. If the key is still in the door-lock tomorrow morning, then I will know that I am asking too much.

Malcolm

It didn't take much deciding on my part. I turned the
key and had a quick walk round the apartment (I
don't know how to call it: Elizabeth's? Studio?
Rooms? Next door?) just to get a sense of the scale of
what Malcolm was asking me to take on. I didn't
want it to get in the way of any writing – but then
maybe it would throw up writing ideas.

There were around forty canvases. Different sizes,
different styles. There was the trunk – full, but not so
big that it would take too much sifting through.

Malcolm,

*I have taken the key and will do what I can to at least
make a start on the things in the room. If I need to ask
or check anything, I will drop you a note. Nothing
will be thrown away. Nothing will be changed. I will
simply do a bit of sorting through and a bit of
thinking around what Elizabeth has left. I will get
back to you before doing anything else. She did leave
those things to you not to anyone else, so she wanted
you to be the final arbiter.*

*You obviously meant a lot to her, as she did to you. It
will take time to come to terms with the absences, but
I am sure that time will come. Meanwhile you can*

trust me to do what I can to help over the next week or two.

Donald

When I had posted the note under Malcolm's door and settled back down to some writing I realised that I had signed it Donald. I never call myself Donald. I am Don.

Don, Donald. At school, at university, I was Don. In New York I am Don to everyone. The only person who called me Donald was my dad. Somehow, here in Vancouver, I have regressed to being Donald. I think this was because the rental agreement wanted my full name. Maybe slipping to being Donald again is OK. Maybe I am good with trying out a different persona for a while.

Variations on names act as aliases, allowing people to be different sides of themselves. How about the others?

Margaret: Was she ever close enough to anyone to be a Maggie?

Elizabeth, Liz, Lizzie, Beth – so many options for her to slide into and out of: other skins to be tried on for size.

Malcolm, I think, would always simply be Malcolm. I can't imagine him wanting to be called anything else

– and maybe no-one will ever think of calling him other than by his given name.

Raphael: Who knows? 'Raffish' comes to mind…

*

This thing about notes being slipped under doors has a cuteness about it in an age of cell phones, email, Twitter, instant messaging and everything. It has undertones of 'He surreptitiously slipped a note under the door and scuttled back along the dark corridor…'. A lost time of handwritten notes, each word chosen carefully for full effect. Such notes take time to write and allow personality to creep in. Malcolm crafts his notes with an old-fashioned ink-pen on heavy-duty writing paper. I bash out my responses in ballpoint on whatever bit of paper was to hand.

That's the difference between his personality and mine. His era and mine. His sensitivity and my functionality.

*

Another note from Malcolm:

Donald,

Margaret, Elizabeth's daughter, is returning to her finance job in Toronto on an evening flight today. She has asked me, and others from the funeral, to call at the house by early afternoon if we wish to see if there are any contents we want to take away before it gets closed up and emptied.

Will you come? I will be leaving here at 12.30. Knock my door just before then if you are able to accompany me.

Apologies for making yet another demand.

Malcolm

*

Margaret was the only one at the house. It was interesting seeing her close-up. At the funeral she had been stiff, black, dour-seeming. Distant and alone. Uncaring and aloof. Now she was wearing jeans and a sweater. She wasn't exactly friendly but was as welcoming as you might expect given that she had just cremated her mother and was sorting through the family home.

I don't know if she had slept there or booked herself into a hotel. She looked a hotel kind of person to me. How do we make those quick judgements about people? We suss people out in less than ten seconds, but which bits of the brain's networks do that, and how do they know what criteria to use? Must read more on neuroscience.

She swept an arm round the whole place and said we could go anywhere and take anything. There were only a couple of things she had wanted, and she had already taken those.

'Anything else is yours if you want it.'

The house was bigger inside than it looked. One thing that immediately struck me was the huge wooden fireplace – a bit out of proportion to the room. When these houses were built the fireplace was probably the focus – roaring log fires, mantlepiece for favourite ornaments. There was craftsmanship in the fireplace. It wasn't some off-the-shelf thing from Fireplaces-Are-Us. It felt handmade for this house. A particular piece of woodcraft to fit a particular living space.

One room downstairs was modernish – 1980s style, at a guess. The other (What would you call it: the parlour?) was as if it had been untouched since the house was built. There was this dark brown wood panelling up to halfway, all round the walls. There is a word for that.

'Wainscot'. That sounds right, although I have no idea why I should know such a word. There are vague memories of it being connected to a childhood story about a mouse that lived behind some wainscot.

If I were a visiting anthropologist coming to study the culture of house-dwelling in early Vancouver I would conclude that it was all about stocking up on food, getting a roaring fire going, and barricading the mice behind some sturdy wooden panelling.

I followed Malcolm as he went from room to room downstairs. He picked out a few books that he had lent Elizabeth and handed them to me. He didn't seem to want much. There were three or four small ornaments that he selected.

I headed to the stairs, but Malcolm seemed appalled.

'That is Elizabeth's private space. I never went up there when she was alive, and I don't intend going there now she is dead.'

I said that I would take a quick peek at the general layout, since I was interested in old buildings. He headed off to speak to Margaret.

He may not have wanted to intrude upstairs but I felt that that is where Elizabeth might have kept her more interesting stuff. Private stuff. Stuff I didn't have Malcolm's qualms about taking. I could look through it myself – my fee for undertaking the small tasks – and only tell Malcolm if there was anything really important.

The bedroom looked like something from the 1950s, which it possibly was. It was bare and functional. I don't think Elizabeth had much time for trends and fashions.

There was a smaller room that was an office. Margaret had obviously been through things. In one corner were a couple of bundles of papers, labelled 'for shredding'.

The only other things in the room were some roughly-packed boxes of lamps and vases, a small stack of magazines, and a bookcase with a mixed collection of books: Nothing recent; little in the way of fiction. Most didn't connect with my idea of Elizabeth. They felt more like leftovers from a past than anything she used.

I picked out what looked like some old diaries or notebooks and put them in a shopping bag, with Malcolm's books and ornaments.

Back downstairs I got the tail-end of a conversation between Malcolm and Margaret, but it ended abruptly with Malcolm going off into the kitchen.

I decided to pump Margaret a little.

'Will you be doing the place up and putting it on the market – or even moving back in here yourself?'

'Move back: God no. There are too many memories in this place, and not all of them good ones by any means. I moved to Toronto a long time ago and if I came back to Vancouver I would slowly start to die.'

I told her that I'd been at university in Toronto, but she seemed not to be interested.

Up close, I tried to read her character. She looked worn out. She took care of her appearances but there were worry lines on her face. Only natural, I suppose, given the circumstances, but maybe she had worries of her own back in Toronto.

Margaret looked round the room.

'The land is more valuable than the building. There is an interest in period housing but not if they need this much doing to them. A developer would clear it all away and put up a small set of contemporary apartments. We will have to see. I have no emotional attachment to it. I will sell it and forget it. I might wish it were different, but that is how it is.'

That fitted with my impression of her. That is what she would do: dispose of the remnants of the old life here. Shake it off and move on. Forget it all. Not give it, or her mother, any more thought.

If she were a character of mine, what would she do – or, more interestingly, what would she never do?

She looked the sort who would never break the rules; she would be the enforcer of rules. In finance. So, some sort of auditor?

What would it take for her to break the rules that she would never ever break?

Maybe there was one bit of grey area, where someone had a hold over her for some reason, and where she did one small transgression – which opened the door to more pressure, slightly larger transgressions, moral dilemmas, hating herself for what she was involved in but not being able to get herself out of it. A slow drift towards shady accounting and offshore businesses, money laundering.

I wouldn't want to introduce the Russian mobster element. Too obvious these days.

*

Days here are taking on a routine that is different in subtle ways from my life in Brooklyn. I get up when I wake, usually around 7.30ish. First step is to head out to the corner store for the day's newspaper, then on to the coffee shop for breakfast. I scan the paper for any ideas, then head back to the apartment to try to get words on paper.

I try to get three to four hours writing and thinking time. I am then freed up to read novels, wander to the shops, visit the library, go to talks, head out for a beer or two, or whatever.

Each writer has their own routines. That is mine.

Malcolm's requests are starting to cut across the morning writing time, but I don't mind. It feels like research. It has the potential to throw something my way that may be useful. I can get the hours in later in the day if I feel like it.

I haven't minded heading out with Malcolm to attend funerals, to look through trunks, or to sift through house contents at Margaret's behest. It all feels important to him. It all connects back to Elizabeth.

In between being Malcolm's fetcher and carrier, I am an urban wanderer. I have become a city nomad.

It is my new normal.

Can I use some elements of my days' existences, my wanderings about the neighbourhood, and create something from it? In the spirit of not being sure what is true, what is false, and what is, as that woman called it, alternative fact, is it possible to write something that is an absolute fiction but rooted enough in reality to sound true?

This is such a visual city.

I have taken to wandering and taking photos of the public art I often pass. Later, looking through the pictures, replaying memories and trying to get beyond the surface, I write whatever comes to me. I try to make it mysterious, or intriguing.

There is this:

> Clearly a body-part: a torso without arms or feet, missing the head. So, from one angle, it is part of a crime scene … a thing that

demands an explanation of how it ended up like that …

Admittedly this sculptural version wasn't gruesome (no blood, no gore) but its discovery, tucked away in a corner of the hotel lobby, still comes as a shock, an unexpectedness, a fascination, a wish-to-know-more.

The dominant thing about the piece is its transparency, the net effect of the latticework; and yet the whole thing has its own solidity – solid enough to cast a shadow. An ambiguity in itself: that stuff of such substance could be constructed out of openness.

Watching the changing light play in and out of the mesh, there was form and shape and substance retaining a sense of emptiness, of being and not-being at the same time: of being and nothingness. Existing yet not existing; real yet not real.

The very emptiness of its net structure creates something new, something with its own existence – the diffraction patterns that shifts and swirls. Something created out of nothing.

Or this:

The gathering of men seems animated: neighbours chatting amongst themselves. They lure you nearer, tempt you to stay awhile, trick you into passing with them the time that you had planned to spend elsewhere.

'But why rush?' they ask. 'Why move on so hurriedly? Rest awhile, stranger. Linger with us. Have fun. Laugh awhile.'
You end up being transfixed there forever as one more member of that silent, smiling gathering.
One man, looking off into the distance, is bent as if he might at any second spring off, yet there he remains, unmoving and unmovable.
I stood as one of the group. I felt their presence. I held my place directly opposite this one man, staring into his look, daring him to change his expression.
I lost myself momentarily and became one of them.
I snapped back and became one of me.

Or this:

Stanley Park: An English park; a legacy from the colonial governor Lord Stanley; with its Rose Garden and so on – and now simply one stop on the tourist trolley bus route.
There, as one of the focal points, harboured in one of its leafy clearings, a collection of totem poles.
There are eyes everywhere, culled from different places, different communities: relocated to stare out defiantly – challenging me to come to terms with a different history, a different way of interpreting the world. The eyes on the totems are transfixing as if the past wants to hold me in its gaze and assess me as

fit (or not) to stand on those traditional lands. I feel small in their presence.

One particular set of eyes held me.

Where the others looked mockingly or accusingly, these eyes held some compassion. With the sun on my back we looked into each other's gaze for as long as one of us could bear it. I found them hypnotic.

I felt compelled to get a shot of them, without wondering if the eyes were those of a beaver or a bear or whatever, just a shot attracted by the eyes because of the electric blue colouring.

*

There were raised voices in Malcolm's apartment. The door was slightly open. It is only because I halted momentarily, worried that something might be wrong, that Raphael looked up. I expected him to get up and close the door, but he just sat where he was and scooped up a bundle of banknotes which he pushed across at Malcolm. Malcolm was out of sight, hidden by the door, but I recognised his voice. Raphael was claiming that it was rent for the next few months. Malcolm was arguing that the rent had already been paid.

Raphael pushed the money further across. There must have been a couple of thousand dollars.

He was insistent.

'OK, wear and tear then.' He looked at me in the doorway and asked, 'What do you think, Donald? Do I look worn and torn to you?'

Malcolm jumped up and pulled the door further open. 'Stop it now, Raphael. You are embarrassing Donald. You are embarrassing me. You are embarrassing yourself.'

Raphael was not to be stopped.

'You see, Donald. This is what I am: An embarrassment to everyone. Malcolm here, on the other hand, is an unembarrassingly boring man from the quieter suburbs of Edmonton. They have cold blood up there. Colder than the blood of Cubans like myself. Yet, delve around inside him, scratch him hard enough, and he lets loose a very different person – one who wears and tears his way through things; wears and tears away at people; even the people he says he loves.'

Malcolm slammed the door. The raised voices carried on inside. I closed the door of my apartment behind me and the voices disappeared.

*

Toronto, New York; Vancouver.

Each city has its own personality. Each different from either of the other two. They each have their own Unique Selling Points.

They each shape the people who live there.

If Margaret could be alive in Toronto but would slowly die in Vancouver, why was that?

We are products of where we grew up. Give me a child until he is seven and I will give you the man – A Jesuit phrase, but what if it were equally true of places? Locate a child somewhere for long enough and they will never be free of the place.

Was it the quiet, sedate suburb of Edmonton that made Malcolm the quiet, sedate person he is today? And what about me? Did the streets overlooking False Creek give me a certain outlook on life – a foundation, a base layer on which other things got laid down: a further layer from Toronto's university district; a layer from Brooklyn? Can I peel back my layers, onion-like, to reveal more and more detailed influences of place?

And what of Margaret? How has she been influenced by Toronto's financial area? Where else shaped what she is? And what of her early childhood in these shady streets of Vancouver's West End?

And Elizabeth? All that early shifting from place to place, language to language, culture to culture. What did that lay down in her developing personality?

Back to Malcolm: He is a product of place, but I also see him as some hang-on from an earlier time, or as leaking in sideward from some slightly-parallel universe where there is more of a focus on civility, on manners, on gentility.

He seems out of place, or out of time, or both.

If he were in a book he would suddenly find himself materialising in a noisy Sports Bar somewhere on the Lower East Side, not knowing what to make of it all. Intrigued and repelled in equal measure.

*

New York; Vancouver; Toronto. Three cities. If they were three sisters what would they be like?

One would be business-suited; making plans; trying to better herself; ambitious, yet a bit restrained, not making too much of a noise about things.

One would be visually attractive; well-dressed; intelligent with it; loose-limbed and quietly at ease with herself.

The third would be the one staying out late at night; comfortable with noise and jostling along through life– a wayward thing; full of energy and verve, with an uncontrollable, slightly distasteful side.

Miss Vancouver appreciates what she has. Miss Toronto wants more. Miss New York takes what she can.

There may be no truth at all in this, but I have a potential story of three young women growing up in some small town – with their separate and collective plans, desires, ambitions and character. It is something to think about on my daily walks along the waterfront or on the drag up to the library.

I have dated all three city-sisters and I think I prefer the one I am with now – the attractive one, the slightly laid back, down to earth one. The one at ease with herself and with me: gracious, gentle and elegant but able to give a bit of a swirl when needed. Beyond her surface, there is a hidden side – a side that she prefers to keep hidden, a side that needs dealing with, but which adds a dash of complexity, a layer of interest.

Is that my person specification for a girlfriend? Are these the key must-have qualities I would enter as data on some dating site (not that I use those). Is that the mental framework I carry in my head, as a template I subconsciously drop around any woman I meet, in order to make that split-second decision: OK/not OK?

*

Transportation in Vancouver seems intuitive, in some ways, but only when you have the big picture of the city's layout in your head. There are interconnecting systems: buses that give the main coverage; SkyTrain routes that run into the city centre and out again; waterbuses that bob along the main creek, and a good supply of taxis for journeys that don't fit with any of those. I can get anywhere, with ease and in a fair degree of comfort.

I have taken the aquabus from a local jetty across to the strip of land where the Museum is. I have hopped on and off buses and trains.

Most of the time I walk along a few main daily routes.

Occasionally I set myself puzzles – joining up the dots of all the various microbreweries and craft ale bars, then getting around by the simplest route possible. I have been to outlying villages with names settlers could have brought straight out of the historical Scottish Highlands or the English Lake District: Kerrisdale, Edgmont, and sat writing in some neat coffee places. I have arced over bridges out of central Vancouver and headed back in on the SeaBus ferry that gives a great reversal of the usual water-from-the-city perspective.

Back in New York, I would walk around the neighbourhood: shopping, coffees, bars, newspapers, the occasional restaurant. Anything else was by subway. The New York subway system has a bad press but for residents it is straight-forward. There are quirks – the stations where you have to come to street-level, cross, and dive back down to change platform. There are trains that stop and trains that are express. It isn't difficult. You just have to leap in and get used to it.

As a student in Toronto, I didn't feel the need to explore the wider transport network. For me, the city was made up of the University district, the city centre and an occasional foray along Queens. It was a city prescribed by my life then. New York is experienced in terms of my life now. Vancouver just seems like a bit of an adventure.

*

An identity can be constructed and reconstructed from fragments, pieced together in different ways. Identity is constantly able to be made and remade through exploration. We work ourselves out in the practices of everyday life.

For some, the fear of not having an identity recognized in the real world takes second place to a fear of having missed a chance to reinforce an on-line identity. There is a need to be always on; always open to capturing the moment – always reproducing ourselves. If each moment is not recorded, then maybe it didn't really happen. If it didn't happen maybe that person doesn't exist any longer.

*

I made a start on the trunk today. I had left it for a few days. I'm not sure why. Maybe it was some of Malcolm's hesitancy rubbing off on me. I didn't know Elizabeth but, even so, it felt appropriate to have a space between going to her funeral and going through her personal stuff. Not that I believe in ghosts. Not that I imagine her spirit hovering over the lock of the trunk whispering, 'Take great care, young man. You are about to open up a Pandora's Box, releasing into the world all manner of thoughts and feelings that you will never be able to stuff back into this precious trunk of mine.'

I am not even sure that this is her trunk. Surely it is now the inherited property of Malcolm. Potentially, it can even be thought of as being in my care, handed on for a while. My responsibility, so – in a way – my trunk.

I thought that I had better get on with it before there is any note under my door enquiring about how things are going.

In what would, normally, have been the bedroom of Elizabeth's apartment was a trestle table with boxes of art materials on it. I cleared it and put it in the middle of the living room. This was the area she used as her creative space. It felt fitting to lay out her treasures there.

All I can say about the trunk itself is: old, no initials stamped on it (So no ownership issues – It is mine, all mine, temporarily), solid wood frame and brass fittings – sturdy, expensive? The kind of chest I might associate with pirate stories, lost islands, buried treasure, skulduggery (again).

It opens easily enough. No great ominous creaking noises. No clouds of dusts. No genies. A bit of a disappointing experience, to tell the truth.

I tried to be respectful, carefully lifting each item out and putting it in sequence on the table.

Things I found:

A folder of official looking documents: Certificates and the like.

Some bundles of letters, in hand-addressed envelopes, tied with old string (Not with pink ribbon, so not love letters from an old flame?), and quite a few more loose ones.

A patterned box containing some jewellery. The sort any woman would collect over a lifetime.

An envelope of photographs – mostly black-and-white and a few colour ones.

A folder full of newspaper cuttings. Looked as if they were all Vancouver Sun pages from the 1950s, 60s and 70s.

Some catalogues for art exhibitions and a few art magazines – all rather faded.

A small homemade doll, stitched fabric, looking well played with.

One pair of knitted baby boots and a cream crocheted baby cloak.

A folder of typed letters – some on letterheads, some on plain paper.

A rather elegant silk scarf – a bit Art Deco looking in style.

I spread them out on the table, scanned through each thing very quickly, then left them there for another day – a rainy day (almost any day in Vancouver). I'll try to get back to them soon. At least I have an outline inventory should Malcolm wish to know.

Things I did notice whist skimming them:

Elizabeth was, I think, born in 1930, in some town with an unpronounceable name (not one of the well-known cities at least) in Poland. No sign of her marriage certificate, unless I missed it, but a death certificate for a Benjamin Crawshaw (died 1951) and a birth certificate for a Margaret Crawshaw (born mid 1952).

Elizabeth's parents, and her, entered Canada in 1946 - so, yes, war-related migrations probably. Their ship passage and personal details all duly recorded.

A set of envelopes all seemed to be in the same handwriting and were postmarked Toronto – so, I am guessing from Margaret.

Most of the colour photos were of three females – I am guessing they might be Margaret as toddler/young child; Elizabeth in middle age; Elizabeth's mother. Just a guess for now but seems reasonable. The black-and-white ones were of groups of young people. No telling where or when – but they looked happy enough.

*

There was an email from my landlord in New York telling me that the work should be finished on time.

*

There are parallels between my parents and Elizabeth's. Both sets moved from Britain to Canada and had families here. Elizabeth's sailed here at the end of the 1940s. Mine had flown here, as a young couple in the early 1970s, and celebrated their new life by conceiving me quite early on.

Were the two Vancouvers worlds apart? Would the 1970s couple have recognised the 1940s streets of Elizabeth's parents? I am sure that some parts would have been pretty much the same, but a lot of development could take place over thirty to forty years. I might follow that up in the library one day.

What about a young person leaving Vancouver now and returning in just over thirty years' time: How much of today's city will they still be comfortably able to recognise in 2050? It is a third of a century away; a generation away. This is way out beyond the limits of the city's three, five or ten-year plans. It is beyond any Vision for Vancouver.

The one thing that might be predictable (unless global warming turns out to be a blip on a chart) is that sea levels will be rising. By then, maybe all these fitness-focused Vancouverites will be talking about using the Seawall walkway as an outdoor swimming lane.

Down by the Convention Centre is a piece of public art in the shape of a needle. The tip, towering above the viewers today, is meant to show where the water level will rise to. Most of the water-front will become the underwater-front. There will be a bit of the city submerged for ever; Vancouver as Atlantis. There could be tourist helicopter rides above the city followed by dives down to swim in and out of the hotel lobby and the meeting rooms of the Centre. The Lost City.

And what of me? I am in the city of here and now. What will have happened to me by 2050? What bits of me will have sunk without trace?

I wonder if my dad stood on the waterfront harbour having similar thoughts? And what of his dad? Where did he stand and what did he think about?

I never met my grandad Donald, but I have always been grateful for the legacy he left me. It was enough money, to come to me on my twenty-first birthday, for me to not have to take on a regular job. I can pretend that I am a writer. I can do odd jobs here and there – coffee shops, bar work, bits of office temping – enough to pay the rent and buy food. I am one of the precariat - the army of people doing a bit of this and a bit of that, on minimal wages and uncertain contracts – or simply cash in hand.

He was a careful, frugal man by all accounts – a journalist in Manchester – so I am not sure that he would approve of paying me to not get a real job.

According to my Dad, grandad was a very black-and-white person so I'm sure he would have had some opinion on it. I'll never know. He died when I was young. I was here and he was in Manchester. No videocalls, no emailing, no easy telephoning. I remember the occasional letter and a small parcel around Christmas.

Maybe I should have talked about him more to my parents.

No chance of that now, either. Mom died when I was young, and Dad went whilst I was at university, taking the knowledge with them. So, Grandad Donald remains a feeling, a fleeting image, a sense – nothing more – but that is enough to make him real in my mind. I believe I knew him even if I didn't really. I believe he cared about me. I have always had a fondness for the image of him.

I just wish he could have known that. Maybe he did.

I wonder if Margaret thinks about her grandparents – those intrepid journey-makers who put themselves and Elizabeth out of harm's way and in a position where Margaret could be born into some sort of security and relative prosperity. I wonder if she has gratitude for that or if it is a taken-for-granted bit of her history – an auditable set of facts.

She didn't seem to have strong bonds with Elizabeth. Maybe she was at the funeral less to mourn her mother and more to make sure that the mother she had lost contact with was really deceased and that the heritage was passing to her in the form of cashable property. Maybe that is too cruel a view of her.

She certainly seemed lonely. No immediate family except her mother, and some gulf even there. No partner that she mentioned. No buzzing phone as friends checked how she was feeling. Not that I can talk. No regular girlfriend in New York (or anywhere). A small group of beer buddies who meet up at the weekends. Occasional on-and-off friendships that never seem to go anywhere.

Maybe I am too much of an outsider. An observer. A collector of people as images, as potential characters, for what use they might be.

*

A note from Malcolm, but not the one I had been expecting. No query about the trunk. No question about Elizabeth's paintings. That surprises me. I would have thought he would have been keen to know. Maybe he has other things on his mind: Raphael, bundles of cash, comings and goings.

Donald,

Before she left Margaret gave me her email address, but I explained to her that I don't really use email. Any formal emailing about issues to do with this apartment block is dealt with by Sam the caretaker or my brother. For everything else I prefer to write

*properly or to telephone. She was reluctant to give me
her phone number. Maybe she imagined that I might
call her at inconvenient times. She suggested that I
find someone to act as my email secretary. I don't
want to involve Sam. He is fine when it comes to
building codes, noisy neighbours and dumped refuse.
I don't think he is a match for Margaret. I was
wondering if it is yet another small thing you could
take on whilst you are here.*

Malcolm.

I like the guy, but I am beginning to see another side
to him. He glides through life offloading jobs onto
others – in this case me. He seems unruffled and
unperturbed because that is how he manages things.
He outsources things. He passes emotional
responsibilities on to other people. Maybe he has to
do that as the only way he can retain enough
emotional reserves to deal with that Raphael
character. I am still not sure what their relationship is.
They are neighbours not a couple living together. I
don't even see them together much. I think Raphael
was at the funeral to support Malcolm rather than out
of grief for Elizabeth. Malcolm seems to treat
Raphael as the son he never had – and a pretty
wayward son at that. Someone who gives him
heartache but who he can't abandon.

After the funeral he wasn't around much (or, if he
was, I didn't see him) – maybe he was on one of his
mysterious trips; and what was all that with the

shouting and the money and the embarrassment when he did return? He is an uncertain, unstable sort of character. There is something dubious about him. He wants to come and go as he pleases, to have a separate life from Malcolm but the two seem glued together by something. He doesn't appear to offer Malcolm much – maybe he buys acceptance. Maybe he returns with small wads of cash and throws that at Malcolm as a way of buying friendship (or fatherhood of sorts). Maybe he is personally erratic but needs someone who accepts him with all his failings – someone to respect and to rebel against, but not some commitment, not a fixed relationship, not a tying-down.

Malcolm can't say no to Raphael, and I can't say no to Malcolm. Like it or not, I am the email secretary between Margaret and Malcolm.

In New York I had a range of jobs. Here in Vancouver, I came to see if I could be a writer but have already accumulated being trunk sorter; assistant house-clearer; note passer; and now, email secretary.

It wasn't in the lease agreement I signed. It wasn't what I had in mind when I left New York. It has just happened, bit by bit.

That is it now: No more temporary roles being taken on; no more erosion of focus. I need to get to grips with whether or not there is any sort of book in me.

There has certainly been no shortage of stimulation:
A woman possibly dying in Trump's face;
mother/daughter tensions; issues around property
values; what heritage means; saying yes when you
want to say no; childhood memories; street people
and financiers; young rebel/old patriarch; auditor
sliding into corruption; a mysterious trunk and the
secrets that it can reveal; personalities and places; …
no end of possible lines.

*

Apartment blocks: It's not about the blocks but about
the spaces between them … the gaps in which one
might catch a glimpse of something else, something
beyond the sides and edges of the colourful facades.
It is about seeing what is not there rather than
focusing on the obvious. It is about looking in hope,
beyond the normal visibility. Things partially
screened, partly hidden, almost secret. Things that can
only be seen at an angle.

People are boxed in. Each apartment is a box within a
block; each block is a square on a grid of streets; each
local grid arranged to form recognizable zones. I have
wandered round most of them: Gas Town, Yaletown,

Granville, Chinatown, Downtown, even venturing out onto the beginnings of East Hastings. Areas that were all neatly delineated on the tourist map, all segregated onto their own page of the guidebook. Each having its own personality: the spirit of the area. Each seemingly having its own purpose in the daily workings of the city; its own meanings for the people who live and work there – and different ones for people like me, meandering through, leaving each zone to get on with things.

*

I met Malcolm at the entry door, on my way back from another afternoon in the library. He had a bag of groceries. On an urge I invited him in for a coffee and, to my surprise, he said yes.

There was a moment of panic as I tried to think if anything was out of place inside. I expected him to be a bit inspectorial, a bit landlordish, but he was relaxed. He knew I wasn't a party person. He saw there wasn't half-eaten food lying around. There was nothing for him not to be relaxed about. Even so, it was the first time I could describe him as 'relaxed' – or at least relaxed-for-him.

I can't say he was at ease. That might have been a step too far.

He was apologetic. Maybe that is why he said yes to the coffee, so that he could apologise: Sorry for the noise the other day; sorry for the rudeness of Raphael. 'He can be a wayward child sometimes'.

There were also Regrets. A pity I never met Elizabeth. He was sure I would have liked her. Everyone liked her, apparently, even if she was sometimes difficult. She had an abruptness, according to him, that came from wanting things to be right. Once you got past that she was a person you could easily take to.

The conversation moved along OK. Not exactly flowed, but not as bad as I might have imagined.

I asked if I had heard right: Was he born in Edmonton? He talked about early memories of being walked to school dressed in puffed-out suits. It was the coldness of the winters that made him want to move South for warmth and for work. That was when he was around twenty years old. He must now be in his early seventies?

He had seen changes over the years: the comings and goings of shifting populations; the demolitions and new-builds of redevelopment; the changes in culture. He had known Elizabeth through much of that time.

His face changed with each bit of the conversation.

When he was talking about Elizabeth there was a slight smile, a bit of a twinkle in his eye and a calm about his expression. I wonder what she was to him.

She was old enough to be his mother, but it doesn't feel like a mothering relationship. Not a romantic/sexual relationship, or at least I don't imagine it was. I am still puzzled by what compelled him to offer up one of his income-generating apartments as an artist studio for her. Maybe she paid rent but nothing in her house or the trunk suggested that she could afford to run an energy-weak old house and pay market rent for some other rooms. I am not confident enough to ask him about it, but I will sometime soon.

When he talked about Raphael there was pain there – a narrowing of the eyes, a tensing of the mouth, a general stressing in the face and body as a whole. 'A wayward child' he had called him. So, he saw him as the son he never had; saw himself as having parental responsibilities, but clearly not the biological father? What was the bond that made Malcolm put up with erratic comings and goings, wilful behaviours, rudeness? What did Raphael get out of it? A free apartment? If Elizabeth got one, why not Raphael? Someone to worry about him, to care for him, to console him when he returned from transgressing, bearing offerings of cash? I'm interested but I'm certainly not going to ask either of them about it.

Somewhere in his ramblings he mentioned that he was celibate by choice. I can't even remember how it arose in the conversation but, suddenly, there it was: an uncalled-for personal revelation. Was he using it to signal something about his relationship with

Elizabeth, or something about his relationship with Raphael – or was he signalling something to me. Whatever, it had come and gone before I noticed, lost in the next bit of rambling.

It was all a bit of a litany really. More Apologies and Regrets. The next step would have been Atonements, but it didn't slip that way. He stuck with Regrets: how it would be a pity if the old house was torn down to make place for a modern box of apartments.

The same as his father might have done, I thought but would never have said.

Is there a hint of contradiction there? A spot of hypocrisy; of double-think?

*

Raphael is an unknown. I see him on the corridor or collecting the post from the lobby. He always seems to be skulking; furtive; lurking. He generates an air of suspicion. He is subdued – not a hot-blooded Latino. Apart from the time he was raising his voice, shouting in Malcolm's apartment, he seemed like someone wanting to hold things in rather than exuberantly let things out. He seemed to want to be insignificant, to be unnoticed.

He is enigmatic, certainly. I guess he is about my age, but I find him hard to pin down beyond that.

But then, what would I say about myself? What am I?

A half-orphan, whose mother died shortly after giving birth to me. So many people, later, telling me that, of course, it wasn't any fault of mine – which prompted a reverse-logic conviction that something was all my fault, even if I didn't know what. My father did his best by me, but he too is gone. I am alone, a loner, isolated (emotionally and socially) living off past legacies.

Whatever we do, we can't shake off the past. It is buried deep inside us all.

*

Psychology-based tales are the thing at the moment. I'm started to read more on cognitive dissonance, neuroprocessing, schizophrenia, emotional Jeckels and Hydes.

*

Elizabeth's paintings have proved a challenge. I am not a trained artist or any sort of art critic. I know what appeals to me, personally, but that is probably as much about me as anything else.

I have lined the paintings, face-out, along the walls of the two rooms in her space. I can walk round and round, like in a gallery, letting them get into my mind.

There are thirty-three. All different. Some abstract; some more defined – none what you might call figurative or landscape. No still lives, although I get the sense that they are stills from her life as it moved on. Snapshots in paint of something in her head? Fragmentary records of her varying states of mind?

Some look quite recent. Others definitely have a collected-dust look about them.

I have left them there for me to go back to from time to time to see if anything leaps out at me. I might start to group them or order them in some way – search for potential patterns. It will be one way of dealing with them. I don't know what else I can do with them.

The things from her trunk are easier to get to grips with. I have slowly gone through each thing in turn.

The certificates have been easiest.

Shuffled to try to get some historical sequence:

There were several in what I took to be Polish. No idea what those were but they looked like birth/marriage certificates, and maybe Identity Cards; and a document with lots of sections and an attached map with a house outlined in red (probably some record of a house purchase or house ownership).

Two certificates were in the names of Agnieska Chelstowska (with a date in 1899) and Jozef Powalski, (1894). One was dated 1930 and was for Elzbieta Powalski. In all likelihood these were birth certificates for Elizabeth's parents and Elizabeth herself. One gave both parents' names and looked like a marriage record, dated 1927.

There were a few documents in German, all dated 1934. My German is based on a few phrases picked up when, me aged fifteen, an exchange student came to live with a family a few doors away. She was several years older than me. I had a real crush on her, following her around at every opportunity. I think she adopted me as a little friend, a cute mascot. I didn't mind so long as I got to trail along behind her. She was so foreign, so exotic to me. I loved her accent and tried to get her to teach me some German.

These documents were way beyond me, but they could be some form of Residency Permits – photos of two rather haggard looking people, plus an address in Germany – and two more about Arbeit, in the same names, which were most likely Work Permits?

The others were in English. There was an Immigration form in all three names, anglicized to Agnes, Joseph and Elizabeth, giving permission, in 1936, to enter the United Kingdom.

They didn't settle. There were travel documents for a passage from Liverpool to Montreal in 1946. Elizabeth would have been a sixteen-year-old teenager. Her parents would have been forty-seven and fifty-two – midlife disruptions yet again. Another journey; another country; another language; another culture. I hope they were adaptable people. Immigration documents confirmed the same names, dates of birth and countries of origin. Religion was given as Catholic - so not Polish Jews fleeing persecution as I had assumed. It is easy to make links that aren't there.

There was an address in Bolton, Lancashire. Why there? Were there relatives? Was that the gravitational place for Polish Catholics coming via England?

A lot of gaps and puzzles.

Part of my brain was scanning the documents to make sense of them for Malcolm; to flesh Elizabeth out in my own mind. There was another, small editor bit in my brain that was simultaneously reading them as potential puzzles, potential material, potential plotlines to be stored away and made use of:

Older couple, finally blessed with a child, but are forced to leave the small forest village in deepest Poland and trek through snow to reach the German border and start a new life – leaving The Thing behind. Fresh starts, but always looking over the shoulder in case The Big Secret catches up with them.

There was a record of Margaret's birth in 1952. Margaret Crawshaw. Mother: Elizabeth Crawshaw.

Father: Benjamin Crawshaw. Beneath that was a record of the 1951 death of Benjamin Crawshaw. So, Elizabeth brought Margaret up on her own. Not easy now; certainly not easy in those days. Margaret partially abandoned at birth? Margaret left with an intense one-to-one relationship with Elizabeth – everything between them magnified so much more?

The rest of the documents were what might be expected. There were several secondary school reports for Margaret. Girl's Catholic school; good grades across the board; a couple of 'must try harder' comments – in art/music. 'A bit of a loner' was a recurring theme, expressed in different ways but boiling down to someone not fitting in too well with other girls for some reason.

There was a program for Margaret's graduation ceremony in Toronto, with her name underlined in pencil. A high-scoring degree in Economics.

I jumped to the other end of the table: The Art Deco style elegant silk scarf.

What was its history? What story could it tell? What owners had handled it, worn it, shown it off?

There was no way of telling other than letting my imagination run away with things:

The scarf being bought in an elegant shop in central Warsaw, maybe around 1910, by Polish ancestors who were rich enough, or aspirational enough, to be able to buy it. The Great War came along. Society got turned upside-down. In all the disruption, the scarf was clung to as a reminder of that previous age. It was stowed safely as the family travels and adventures started. It was an heirloom, passed down – the only thing left of the past life – stories told as an old woman's hands stroked it. It was handed over with some small ceremony – a treasured link back to where they had come from, who they were. A treasured bit of history.

I momentarily put the scarf round my neck, closed my eyes, breathed in its accumulated scents and imagined past meetings, overheard conversations – family secrets woven into its fabric and no longer able to be teased out.

There was something a bit magical about it and yet, back on the table, it was just an elegant silk scarf.

I suddenly felt as if I shouldn't be there. I was intruding on the secret life of those objects – things that should not be disturbed. Things that needed to be left to rest in peace.

*

Most people who move to Vancouver end up staying. It is a magnet city. It attracts you, draws you in, holds you tight, never lets you out of its grip. My dad, it seems, wasn't most people. He enjoyed Vancouver but moved on. Maybe it was his wife dying. Maybe it was his job. Whatever, after several years I was dragged to Calgary then Edmonton. For me it simply meant trying to make new friends, adapting to new schools, getting lost on new streets.

Dad stayed in Edmonton, but I was still on the move. On to Toronto to go to university. On to New York. And now on (or back) to Vancouver. Does that square a circle? Is it to do with those TS Eliot lines about arriving back where you started but knowing the place for the first time? Is this my chance to understand myself?

Is that why I am here?

*

There was a circular set of emails around some of my neighbours in New York. One had emailed a group of us, confirming that work was indeed underway. That started a bit of a discussion. There were rumours that the landlord is hoping to put up the rents once the work is done. There were questions about where we stand legally if that is the case. There was a bit of back and forward – opinions and anger. I stayed out of it. Better to wait until there is something definite. A couple of people offered to email the landlord on our behalf to get some clarity.

*

I have a photo on my phone that I have absolutely no memory of taking. Yet I must have done. There it is in the memory, sandwiched between a shot of the Steam Clock on Water Street and a later shot of a strange little statue of Emily Carr.

I am not even sure what it is. It could be steps, or shelves, or balconies. It could be a picture of things high up, from below – or maybe that is some illusion. There are diagonals; there is repetition; there are lines of light, blocks of darkness, hints of colour and pattern to break the monotony. I can see all that, but still have no memory of taking it.

I remember sitting in the Starbucks next to the steam clock. I remember the longish walk down to the jetty and the bobbling little boat across to Granville Island. I got a bit disoriented trying to find a way back up to the bridge to start the short trek back. It was there that I came across this statue of a woman, a donkey and a monkey. The plaque explained all. I remember stopping, reading.

I remember Starbucks and the clock. I remember the bobbling boat. I remember the weather, the seagulls, the flyover, the traffic. I remember the statue.

I remember everything: So why have I no memory of taking this shot? I find it incredulous that I have the tangible evidence of having done something that my brain has no memory of me having done. Scary.

*

I plucked up courage to tackle the bundles of letters. In the string-tied bundle, the first letter I opened was brief. It was a letter from Margaret to her Gran, Elizabeth's mother. Margaret writing, not to her mother, but to her mother's mother. Worse than that: Margaret thanked her Gran for letting her write.

I can't stop her intercepting my letters to you. I can't stop you sharing them with her, but I trust you. You know why I can't write to her.

She thanked her Gran for being at the graduation.

Even though things are strained, it was good that Mom came as well. Maybe we can patch things up. Not yet though. The gulf is too wide. I don't think we will ever be whole in the way other moms and daughters are. It is OK whilst you are around. Look after yourself.

There were other letters on similar lines:

If I can't write to you I don't know what I'd do. I have to write some feelings down and you are the only one

I trust to read them properly. There are others here at university but they would make a lot out of everything and I don't want that, I never want you to do anything, just be there and read them. It helps knowing that I have someone there who understands things.

There were letters every few weeks. Some quite personal. Some about her courses. Some about things in Toronto. There were long gaps, either because Margaret hadn't written or because the ones in the bundle were selected ones – ones kept for one reason or another; others being deemed not worth keeping and thrown away?

The loose letters were a mix. Amongst them were replies from Elizabeth's mother to Elizabeth; and letters that Elizabeth had sent to her mother. Written in ink. Elizabeth's in a flowing cursive hand; her mother's more sturdy.

I copied fragments from different letters:

Postmarked 1947.

Mother: I hope you understand why I left and why I want to live in the colony. I feel that I am more able to find my place in this new life. Bolton wasn't easy but here, in Canada, in Vancouver, everything seems possible.

There is so much creativity here. I am safe and well. There is no need to worry. You are my mother, you will worry whatever I say. I will come to see you soon. Love Elizabeth.

Dear Elizabeth

I was so pleased to get your letter. Yes, I worry. Why should I not worry, I am your mother.

I can't understand why you left, and why so suddenly. It's not as if we argued. We never argue. You did leave, though, and you must have had good reason. You will share that with me when you are ready. It hurt then, and it hurts still. We have always tried to give you a good life. Did we not travel halfway across the globe for a better life? We only wanted you to be happy.

You were unhappy in Bolton but I really believed that here would be different. I didn't think it would be different in this way. You can always come home, you need to know that. Your room is ready for you, even if you are not ready for it just yet. Keep writing. Visit. Be happy but do not be a stranger to your family.

Your loving mother

Postmarked 1948.

Mother: Life is good and I am happy. People are kind. Ben, the Ben I told you about last weekend, is good for me. He is one of the new group of artists. They are being called the new Group of Seven, although there are more than seven here at the moment. I know you worry and I can't stop that. Nor would I want to. Love Elizabeth.

Dear Elizabeth,

I was so pleased that you came at the weekend. I don't pretend to know why you stay in your ramshackle cabin, but it was obvious that you are happy. Thankyou again. We are here if you need anything.

Your loving mother

Dear Elizabeth,

I had a Christmas letter from your uncle in Bolton. He hopes you are well. He has been ill himself. It will be good to have you here at Christmas. Benjamin is invited. I don't know if he will want to come, or if you will want to bring him. To be honest, I don't feel that I know you at all at the moment.

Your loving mother

Postmarked 1949

Mother: You are always welcome to visit, you know. It's not some group of dangerous revolutionaries. There are only a few people, almost all creative, some musicians, some artists. We all care for each other. We try to live simply. It is the most exciting thing that has happened to me. It is more exciting than the trip out to Canada. It is far more interesting than anything in the cold and damp of industrial Lancashire. I am so glad we moved from there. It had nothing to offer but grey and more grey. No artist would survive that. Here there is the sparkle on the water, the swooping gulls, the colour and movement all around our wooden buildings on the shoreline. Love Elizabeth.

Dear Elizabeth,

It was kind of you to come home and tell me face-to-face. My immediate reaction may have given away my deep feelings and I hope it wasn't too strong. Of course we will come. Of course I am happy for you. Why should I not be happy, you are my daughter. It was still a surprise to hear that you are getting married. Your father and I married late in life and we were just not ready for our little girl to be already taking such a big step.

I have some fruit from the garden that I will bring round to you. I was going to make jam, but you look as if you need fresh fruit to add to your foodstore.

I will have to start looking out for something to wear.

Your loving mother

(Later in 1949)

Mother: I know you are disappointed in me. I am not the daughter you wanted. I hope you are not too frustrated by it all. I saw your face when I told you about the wedding. I could tell that you didn't approve. I know you would have wanted a good Catholic wedding with lots of extended family there, but we don't have a family here. My family will always be you and Dad, but I also have this other family of artist friends. The fact that it was a small and simple ceremony would be another disappointment. Still, it was lovely to have you there. Love Elizabeth.

Dear Elizabeth,

The wedding ceremony was lovely. There is no need for an elaborate church when a simple one will do. God is in both. Benjamin seems a good person. I am sure that he will take care of you every bit as much as we tried to do. I could see the love radiating between the two of you.

Your father is always grumpy at ceremonies. Pay no attention to him. He doesn't fit easily into social events. He is getting more withdrawn, actually. I don't worry. Well, that is not true really. I do worry about him. I just try not to let him see that I am worried. We will be fine. We have always been fine.

Your loving mother

Postmarked 1950

Mother: The group of us went on a road trip to Seattle last week. There was a bit of hassle at the border for a couple of people, but nothing serious. It was fun. I sold a lot of my stuff so this week I am going to the markets looking for clothes to replace the ones that have got beyond repairing. I also like to have at least one thing that is a bit expensive, a bit different. There aren't many occasions when I feel like wearing something special but I will find something to wear for when I come to visit for your birthday. Love Elizabeth.

Dear Elizabeth,

I was so happy to see you and Benjamin for my birthday. The scarf is lovely although it must have cost you more than you can afford. I will treasure it.

You looked well and healthy. Life is being kind to you and that makes me content.

Your loving mother

(Later in 1950)

Mother: *Thanks for visiting and bringing the knitted blankets. There was snow in the air but the secluded hollow gives us shelter from the cold. The cabin is fairly well insulated. The blankets are really welcome though. I will think of you as I snuggle down all cosy and warm. Come again when you can. Love Elizabeth.*

Dearest Elizabeth,

Benjamin was lovely at the funeral. I know that he found your Dad difficult but the things he said in memory of him were just right. I have had letters from friends here. I have written to folks back home and in Bolton but don't expect an answer yet. Dad's brother will be so upset to get the news. I have tried to reassure him that Dad died peacefully in his sleep.

Neighbours have brought food, but I really can't face conversations with them. They are sensitive enough to just smile, offer the food and leave.

You mustn't worry about me. I will get through things. We have always got through things. Until now I have had someone helping me to deal with life. Now I will deal with things on my own.

Call to see me when you can.

Your ever-loving mother

Postmarked 1951.

Mother: *I am devastated. Ben died overnight. Last night he was fine. Today he is dead. They think it was a heart attack. Sorry to be so blunt but life seems blunt just now. Sorry to write and not tell you in person, but the reality is that I can't talk to anyone at the moment. I will come to see you maybe tomorrow. Elizabeth.*

Dearest Elizabeth,

My poor child, I don't know what to. You looked so small and sad when I hurried round to see you.

You are naturally feeling devastated at the moment and I can offer platitudes like 'It will pass...', 'Give it time ...', 'Things will get better ...' but losing the love of your life leaves a space that is impossible to fill. We are widows together, so suddenly. That seems such an odd thing to have to write, but life seems at odds with itself just now. Your loving mother

(later in 1951)

Mother: You may not like this, so I will straight out with it. I am pregnant. You are going to be a granny. I hope that you can be happy for me and the baby, however things turn out. Love Elizabeth.

The writ has been dropped for the Provincial elections here in a month's time.

The gloves are off from the start – allegations about this and that. Announcements are already coming thick and fast. Slates of candidates are being worked on. Electioneering platforms are being put out.

Much of it is standard stuff. One side wants to raise welfare rates; for another side it's all about creating more jobs.

Some is sheer opportunism. The news has been full of a story about the high level of deaths of kids in care, and immediately one of the parties was all over the issue.

*

I have been thinking a lot about cities and writing about cities. For any city there is constant change and constant renewal, with some people left always trying to pin their city down in order to understand it and other people left behind, covered over, no longer seen.

I have also been dreaming about cities.

Maybe all that can come together: Some made up accounts of made up dreams of made up cities.

Something like:

I often dream of cities. Usually there are battlements and buttresses: towering slabs of red sandstone or flinty blocks of grey granite. In the air there is sometimes a forbidding-ness, a forbidden-ness; causing a hesitancy in how I might plan my approach. Usually I am on horseback or on foot; sometimes in armour, sometimes in rags. I am always travelling alone but as I look across the barren space there are always black threads shuffling forward, mingling, merging in small scuffles of dust.

I urge myself forward. Threads converge, funnel onto the drawbridge, hunch under the portcullis, sweep on past the faces safe in their guardhouse. We surge further, in anticipation, spreading, exuberant; on into the twisting streets, the narrow alleyways. We move through souks; taking in every trace, every sight, every sound, every smell that the city offers.

I push my way through, jostling, until I am in the Great Square. I stand, taking it all in. At that instant I become the city and the city becomes me.

Here the stream has thinned to small knots of people scattered across the vastness of the Square. Families look around in wonder. Children dash from one excitement to the next. They are newcomers. I could try to tell them what will happen, but they probably wouldn't listen to me.

The city will draw them closer. They will be bemused by the ins-and-outs of it all, by the twists-and-turns of it all. They will be drawn in by faded memories;

sucked into holes in the city's fabric as it unrolls before them. They will lose themselves there for a while. I can tell them all that, but they will still need to discover it for themselves.

I Leave them behind with their anticipations and their unknowns.

I start walking. There are a few people heading the same way. Occasionally I pass stalls of fresh fruit and bottled water. I am joined by a woman. She keeps looking across, as if certain that she has seen me somewhere before. I am just as certain that I have never met her. We walk on in silence. She holds back, a few paces behind, but from time to time I slow suddenly so that she comes into view. She is tall, in a red flowing dress. Attractive but with an awkwardness about her. I speed up again and she matches my stride. For a while we are side by side in our silence. Suddenly, I look across and she is gone. I check my pockets. Everything is there. I walk on alone, head high, eyes on the distant lights.

I get closer as dusk comes in slants.

Or:

The mist settles into patterns. The patterns coagulate. This is what I have come to see. This is what is different every time.

I am in a room. White walls, white ceiling, white floor. It is an empty box. There are window spaces but no glass. There are doorways but no doors. I can see through to a similar room beyond and another beyond that. Similar but not identical. They are boxes linked to boxes. Not vertically as in an apartment block; not horizontally as in a row of terraced houses. There is a higgledypigglediness about the construction, as if the boxes were driftwood nailed in place.

The place looks patched together, put together hurriedly. Thrown together; pieced together – not quite fitting, not quite matching up. There is a sense of something once started but which has now stopped. I am in the partially abandoned carcass of some community whose lives have been left behind, stranded in place and time as things press on.

Glancing through one of the window spaces I think I catch a distant glimpse of scaffolding and half-complete buildings. It must be an illusion for when I look steadily there is nothing there.

The whole place is suspended, slowly rotating in a white, misty breeze: a tissue floating quietly in the air. It is delicate, fragile: A world of its own. I feel as if, all around me, something is being made out of nothing. It is hard to tell whether this is a place that has grown and spread, or a place that is slowly falling in on itself from stuff that no longer exists.

Whatever it is, or once was, this is a washed-out, run-down place; a discarded place. It is not total dereliction; not absolute abandonment. There is a lingering hope of return. In one room there are chairs. I can sit on them.

As I move from one room to the next I think I can hear voices. Voices that seem powdery, like dust. Voices whispering to me from somewhere in the past. They want to tell me about things that happened. They want me to know.

They don't disturb me even if I have the feeling that I have disturbed them. They whisper quietly but leave me to roam, room to room to room. I stand at a place where the voices seem loudest. Even here they are barely whispers. When I listen, it feels more like people breathing but when I concentrate there are words, sentences; an urgency of feelings.

They are telling me about a time before the city, before the displacement. They want me to know that they were happy. They want me to know that they are still there, underneath everything. If people like me dig down beneath the city life we can uncover them. Our delving will allow them to talk to us. They feel that they have been silent for too long. Maybe they hope that I will be able to write it all down or tell other people. Maybe they are longing to find a voice. Maybe that is why I am here.

One growing election issue is the number of homeless in British Columbia, specifically in Vancouver. It is all over the newspapers because of a well-timed report.

'Homeless Numbers in MetroVan jump 30%'

Apparently, there are 3,605 in the greater city area. High housing prices and high rental charges are a big part of the problem – a problem that is increasing faster than solutions are being found.

With each decade people are being pushed down the housing chain, into smaller and less suitable properties – with people at the bottom of the pile living in vehicles or on the street.

As usual, every political platform is pledging 'Something Must Be Done' or 'We Will Tackle Things', but always short on detailed practicalities. All sizzle with little or no steak.

The folder and newspaper cuttings from Elizabeth's rooms, were a mixed bag.

Some bank statements. Always in credit, not by much. Elizabeth was a careful woman. She paid her way through life. In more ways than one.

Mostly they were bills and receipts, going back years, for repairs to the roof, for new windows, for repainting, for fixing a blocked drain, for gutter-clearing and work cutting back the garden. They recorded the endless cycles of renovations and patching-ups that any old house demands. For Elizabeth, they represented a steady draining of finances, and probably a steady flow of irritations and worries. Did the house, with its endless needs, drain her emotionally?

Margaret has the house now. Will it drain her? Financially? Emotionally? She seems able to shrug off such things.

There was a letter ordering Elizabeth to make a Court appearance in March 1975. It doesn't say what for.

There was a solicitor's letter referring to the death of her husband. There was mention of an attachment (missing) that she had to sign and send back, authorising release of funds from his Will. Plus some documentation around life insurance payable on death.

There was a clip of work contracts for different places:

Start dates for work in shops.

A termination letter from the early 1990s: 'As you know, our retail store is relocating to bigger premises. We are sorry you feel that the new journey time is too long given your caring commitments. We have always valued your work with us and will supply any references needed for future employments you may apply for.'

Others along similar lines tell a similar story. Elizabeth was a trusted and efficient worker, always part-time, sometimes retail and sometimes hotel work.

When Agnes got sicker, Elizabeth gave up work altogether.

Until then she had consistently worked hard and tried to do her best for Margaret and for Agnes. One female sandwiched (squeezed? suffocated?) between two others – a common enough tale but one that, in this case, was unique to her.

Will come back to all of this later.

*

Two old guys on the bus over to North Vancouver:

'Did you hear that Trump guy on TV? He sure has his own way of talking. Brash, I'm telling you, and clumsy with his words.'

'Didn't much take to that other one though. The woman. She came over as all entitled. She seemed smug, and arrogant with it.'

'That was the choice in front of voters: Brash Clumsiness versus Smug Arrogance.'

'Fly-by-nighty wheeler-dealer: self-interested to the core versus In hock to big business: vested interests pulling the strings.'

'No real choice. People voted all the same. Half for one, half for the other. That's America I suppose: 50% brash clumsiness and 50% smug arrogance.'

'Remember that couple in the motorhome last year. Pulled up at the local grocery store; not only wanted to pay for everything in US dollars but also wanted the change in US money. Can you believe them?'

'Stands to reason that some must be normal. That's what normal means. It's just that a chunk of what's normal in that country is extreme anywhere else.'

'I hear that, since the election, they are coming over our Southern border just to get away from it all. Applying for Canadian citizenship and all.'

'One program headlined it as 'Trump Dodging'. Like draft dodging without the draft.'

'Maybe we should build a wall.'

'Build a wall, and make the US pay for it.'

'I don't recall that cropping up as an election slogan here in BC.'

'Not yet. Maybe we should suggest it as a knock-out line for the Liberals, they sure as hell need some good lines.'

*

Elizabeth's notebooks. Four of them, a bit battered. Not diaries, as such, just a set of notebooks written out in Elizabeth's handwriting. Rescued from the house. Rescued from Margaret.

One notebook was mostly recipes, household calculations, notes on health regimes, a few sheets folded in here and there.

One was completely filled with sketches and ideas for paintings.

Scattered through another were entries that were reminders and to-do jottings:

- *Opening soon: The Western Front. An artist-run centre. Find out more.*
- *Buy new curtains?*
- *Morris and his concrete poetry. Article in newspaper says 'part of mail art network'. What was that? Does it still exist? How do you get into it?*

- *Next week. Jeff Wall at Nova Gallery. Who can I go with? Who will sit with Mom?*
- *Emily Carr Art School is heading over to Granville Island. It has an outreach programme and summer school. Find out more about this.*
- *Mom. Doctor's. Wednesday 11.30*
- *Vincent Trasov is running for mayor as Mr Peanut – Dressed as a peanut! Find a way to meet him.*

The thickest one had pages filled with snippets about people.

Some of these were clearly individuals she knew from somewhere. Others may simply have been people she had read about or heard about. It wasn't always easy to tell.

There were jottings on people in Vancouver life: Politicians and what they were proposing, and her views on that – usually strong, usually opposing. From her notebook I would have her down as left-to-middle in her politics. Fierce in her views but with an underlying gentleness and appreciation of others' standpoints.

There were quotes attributed to people she met on the street, or to friends of hers, or to famous people – as if she were storing up potential mottos to live by.

Some pages were taken up with extended thoughts:

What's going on at the School of art? In the rush to be modern, the School has gone down a route where grades have almost been eliminated; classes are being opened up to almost anyone (That could be me; that can be me); and learning is done through self-directed projects. Art is stretched further and further: performances, dance, poetry – Is there no limit?

Page after page was filled with her notes on artists and what their shows were about, ideas that she agreed with or disagreed with. In the middle of it all there were personal cries from deep inside herself:

Am I getting left behind? They are all artists. I am what? A washer and feeder of someone who can be difficult, but who I love all the same. A mother and worrier about someone who can definitely be difficult, but who I equally love all the same. That sums me up.

The outsiders I knew who are now on the inside are all men. I am left looking in from the outside, a woman.

There is a meet-up next week at the Art School on Gender and Art. Can I go? Only if I get someone to fill in for me here. It's like that pin-badge I bought in Seattle all those years ago:

"I will join the Revolution when I can get a babysitter"

One long entry was about an old friend of hers having an exhibition:

John has finally got his own exhibition. It is, admittedly, at a small and out-of-the way gallery but it is a real show in a real gallery. He deserves it after all he has been through. He was kind to me in those days out on the mudflats, beyond the reach of the city authorities. His show looks back to those times, seeing them as his springboard for all that he has done since. He even called it An Intertidal Event.

When we met, all those years ago, he had already had an interesting life.

I think it was his early hardships that made him show such kindness and generosity to me. Looking back, I see that has was also being very protective. He saw me as a vulnerable teenage girl dwelling amongst a mixed bag of characters. He kept an eye on me. Without me knowing, I think he also warned some of the men off me.

He would come by daily just to see how I was and if I needed food or other stuff. He was the opposite of my father. He was relaxed, a bit carefree. He didn't suffocate me.

He was a great teller of tales. Even now, after all these years, I can recall his expressions as he told me details about the depression years. It must have been grim, all those men living out at the city dump.

He made the characters come alive. The smart one with one leg, trouser pinned at the knee, always with a tie and waistcoat, crutching himself precariously on the timber walkways across the mud-swamp.

The old guy, flat cap, bundle in hand, going out relentlessly day after day, hunting for a job and never dispirited when he got back each afternoon without one. He was the one with the talent for turning discarded stuff from the dump into something useful like a stove or a lamp or a chair. He knocked things together in the evening then just left them out for whoever needed them.

He was so visual in the way he described things. You could feel the trails through thickets of willow, see washing drying on hedgerows. You could sense the claustrophobia and comradeship. People of all nationalities living as some world united by unemployment. He claimed that some went on to be famous politicians or well-known union organisers.

He claimed that he used to tell visitors that in the camp 'there are two hundred men and two million flies'.

He gave things enough animation to lodge them in your mind as memorable images. Homes made of barrels and packing cases, so low that you had to crawl to get inside. A timber, corrugated iron and tar-paper shack was home to fourteen men. He said he started there but couldn't stand the snores and the farts.

He moved between camps on the old Hastings Sawmill, on some railway land, and under the Georgia Viaduct. Always on the move because of sweeps by the authorities trying to close down the camps.

'But where could people go? What were the people to do?' he used to ask me, as if I, a bit of teenage vulnerability, could help him out with an answer.

He had been born in the West End before the boom, when the place was still rolling hills, brambles and tree stumps. After his time in the camps he ended up back at the West End when it was beatnik: a forty-year-old in with a crowd of performers and artists. I lost touch with him after that.

When I saw him at the launch he couldn't believe it was me!

His show is full of assemblages. The pieces are mostly made from scorched wood.

He was still spinning stories about how all the works had lines back to those days of knocking scraps of things together in the camps.

'I was trying to make meaning of stuff then, and I am still trying to make meaning of stuff now,' he said.

I told him I loved it all. He seemed touched.

One entry, dated 1972, was more personal:

So, my daughter has moved out. I am in no position to complain, after all I did the same thing at around her age. I didn't give much thought to any grief I might be causing. I didn't feel the need to explain myself to my parents. They were my parents. If it was the right thing to do, they would understand. If it was the wrong thing to be doing, then that would be their fault for the way they brought me up. It was me, selfishly, doing just what I wanted. So, yes, I understand intellectually but it still hurts inside.

I hear about what she is doing because she writes to her gran. Mom tells me what Margaret has told her. It is as if she is telling me things about when I abandoned her. She angles it so that she is talking about my daughter but appears to be talking about me.

Tucked in the back of the notebook was a fragment of a typed letter.

...... You told everyone that the baby came late. You told us, me included, that it was a blessing, a memory of Ben, a result of his last act the night before he died. I have recently wondered, did the baby come late or was that your cover-story.

Was the baby mine?

You left the colony and I moved away. We went different ways and I gave it no more thought.

Why now? I thought I saw you at one of my shows in Vancouver but, by the time I had shaken people off, you – if it was you - had gone. I am in Vancouver for a few days, organising another show. One of the wonders of the internet is that you can track people down, even if they don't particularly want to be found.

We are both old. I find myself spending more time mentally tying up loose ends. Which got me thinking about us, about that one night, and about the possibility of the baby being my child. The baby will now be in his/her (?) sixties, which is far too late for me to even think about entering their life.

I am not even sure why I am writing.

I think of you often, but I am far from sure what you think of me. Maybe you think I took advantage of you.

You had lost Ben almost a month before but were obviously still upset. I used to sit with you, nothing more, just holding your hand and letting you cry. That one night you wanted more, you wanted holding, you seemed to be OK with what we did. If you think it was wrong, I am sorry. There was never any intention to take advantage.

I am not trying to resurrect the past. That is long gone. I simply wanted to make some contact and leave it there, leaving it for you to do what you wish.

You always were the clear-headed one out of us all. That, and strong willed. You will do what you feel is best for you, I know that.

Typed letters don't give you the same opportunity to judge the writer's character. This one tried even harder to conceal anything about the writer. The address had been torn from the top and, if it had once been signed, any name had been torn from the end.

This was a letter that Elizabeth had deliberately chosen to keep but had even more deliberately chosen to keep secret.

*

Malcolm was in a strange mood last night. I think he just needed someone to talk with. There was no surreptitious note. He brazenly, for him, knocked the door and even more boldly asked if I wanted to talk over a couple of glasses of wine.

The couple of glasses got to nearer a couple of bottles. He asked about me. He wanted to tell me something of himself. Underneath it all, I sensed an urge to talk about Raphael.

Key facts as I recall them after a heavy night's sleep:

He was religious once, 'severely lapsed'. His parents were Church People – the kind to make him what he is: quiet, considerate, cultured, compliant.

There wasn't much he remembered from childhood: Praying for lost souls, handing out leaflets; the unfriendliness of school, the bullying. The meetings about things from faraway times, faraway places, faraway lives – a strange exotic, set against the severity of the religion's demands. There were enforced visits to galleries, museums, the occasional theatre.

His father, particularly, was formal. There was a paternal stress on morality, with long lectures on the sin of sex outside marriage and the virtue of celibacy. His parents died just as he might be developing any interest in sex. Celibacy became a habit, then a way of life rather than a moral choice. He ceased to think about any other options, any possibilities.

After his third glass of wine, Malcolm got morose – hinting at something deeper. Times that he wouldn't – couldn't – speak about. Times he tried not to think about – something there in his memory, but not there at the same time – something painted over, whitewashed away, something that possibly never even really happened?

He moved away from Edmonton to get free of that background. He thought he could shake it all off by moving to somewhere a bit freer. The old religion still had him by the throat, even so.

Raphael (like me) had simply turned up one day looking for an apartment. He was a few years older than me, coming up to fifty. 'A strange age for any man' according to Malcolm, but I had no idea what he meant by that.

Raphael always was going to have an interesting background. He had described himself as Cuban during that little shouting set-to in Malcolm's apartment. All false, according to Malcolm.

'Poor Raphael. A bundle of lies from start to end.'

His mother was Metis. His father was possibly a sailor. Maybe even a Cuban sailor, but that didn't make Raphael Cuban, did it?

He was born in Montreal. He was Canadian. Not even sure that Raphael was his real name. Maybe he wanted to identify with a father he didn't know.

From what Malcolm could piece together Raphael never went to school and claimed to have been taken in by a Jesuit priest who thought he was a religious prodigy. He now 'wanted to have the childhood that was stolen from him'. He said he had lived in Winnipeg but, later, denied ever having been there. Claimed he had a degree, from the University of Life. After a while it became impossible to sort fact and fiction.

Raphael was a good tenant, no problems there.

He would go to Malcom every time he had problems, which was every few weeks.

He would go off, never telling Malcolm where. He would always come back after a few days. Sometimes with bruises from a beating. Sometimes with wads of cash. They would always argue; Raphael would always break down and cry; Malcolm would always console him – then the whole sequence would repeat several weeks later.

Malcolm said that he met Elizabeth because they both used the same corner coffee place. She would sit at the same table, writing and sketching in her notebook. He didn't disturb her; they simply nodded to each other in recognition.

Elizabeth split her time between caring for Agnes, holding down a series of part-time jobs and sitting in the café trying to protect a tiny bit of time for herself. Protecting that space was one reason she didn't speak to Malcolm for a long time.

When they did talk, things flooded out on both sides. They found it easy to be with each other. Easier because they had no other connection. There was a confessional feel to it, Malcolm said – meeting at a set time, three times a week, letting stuff out and feeling better for it.

Malcolm told her about his upbringing in Edmonton. Elizabeth told him about arriving in the UK and moving on to Vancouver. She talked about the art colony. She told him about Margaret being a good child who was embarrassed by her background.

There were big gaps in what Malcolm knew about Elizabeth's life, but he did know that she had been involved in all sorts of things. He also knew that she had really wanted to be a painter, and that the others in the colony thought she had real talent – but all of that got shelved when Margaret came along, and when Agnes needed so much caring for. Eventually, he offered her the apartment to paint in, bought her some canvases and paints and found someone to sit with Agnes for an afternoon a week.

When Agnes died, Elizabeth poured herself into painting.

It was clear that Malcolm wanted to do the best by his friend. The problem, as ever, is how do you know what is best? There can be no controlled trial where you test out all options at the same time then go with the one that works best. The only reassurance is that whatever decision gets made is the best one at the time, whatever the real-life outcomes, because people rarely willingly make a choice that doesn't feel right in that moment.

*

Earlier, I spent a long time watching the change of light and shadow on a small length of fence.

The lines; the edges; the transitions; the patches of light in the shade and patches of shadow in the light; the hard, fixed lines of the wooden slats interplaying with the fuzzier shifting lines of shadow; the straights and the arcs; the ambiguities of it all.

When I stopped watching I realized that I had spent more than an hour there. Amazing how long you can spend watching a line of light move across a background.

*

Elizabeth's photos

Black and White photos:

1. Three young women; road sign in German; snowing. Waving at photographer (who was therefore a friend?).
2. I guess Agnes and her husband. Sunny day with harsh shadows. Could be anywhere.
3. Woman and girl aged around eleven in school uniform: Terrace of houses all identical; bleak looking place (could be Bolton?). There are

factories in the background – but factories are factories are factories …

4. Woman and girl (as in other photos) giggling together outside a house that is unmistakably Elizabeth's,

5. Young woman (Agnes, I am sure) looking back over her shoulder in a doorway. Not either of other places in photos. Has an Eastern European feel about it, but I'm not sure what I mean by that – maybe the exposed, external wiring and junction boxes.

6. Not Margaret. Photograph is slightly creased at corner and is old. Likely to be young Elizabeth. Could be young Agnes but I think not.

More black-and-white ones in an envelope:

Various groups of young people; different settings. A recurring one being water-side scenes – splashing, swimming – all of them smiling. All the time smiling. Smiling for the camera, or only photographed when there were smiles all round? We know that photographs can be unreliable sources of evidence, and that was even in the days before Photoshopping. Darkroom diddlings could make any picture out of next to nothing.

Several stood out:

- A van. Six people lined up alongside it. A sign 'Seattle Steaks and Ribs'. They look a likeable lot – scruffy, relaxed, happy...

- Snow. A young woman lying spread-eagled, as if just dropped out of the sky. Could well be young Elizabeth. One of the faces lined up next to the van in Seattle.

- Fencing, posts, ropes with paintings strung up. An outdoor informal exhibition? A sale? Can't see the detail of the paintings except that they all appear to be abstracts, blocks of light and shade.

- A man staring out from next to a cabin, half hidden in trees (cabin and man, both). The unusual thing is that there was no smile – not even a hint that he had been smiling or was about to smile: no sense that he even could smile. There was a haunted look on his face; a hunted look. Gaunt – that's the word. Gaunt, with deep shadows under his eyes – not mascara – poverty, hunger.

Colour photographs:

1. Close up of a teenage girl – same person as in school uniform in the other photo; and unmistakably Margaret.

2. Margaret at her graduation – formally posed in graduation gown
3. Some shots of Elizabeth and several other women of similar age (Could be neighbours?)
4. Various shots of same three people: Agnes, Elizabeth and Margaret – from Margaret as toddler; Margaret on her first day at elementary school; in high school uniform; setting off somewhere (To university?). Always Margaret in the foreground, the other two as supports – one on each side.

*

Margaret emailed.

She is in town and wants to discuss a few odds and ends. Malcolm dithered about going to meet her; not going to meet her. He opted for not going (No real surprise there) and assumed that I would go (Again, no real surprise).

I met her for coffee. She was different.

She was far from that scrunched-up overly-stiff person at the funeral. She leaned comfortably in her chair. She looked me in the eye. She was relaxed and charming. At one stage I had to remind myself that she was my mother's age, if my mother had still been alive.

She was the opposite of the closed-off person I had her down as a couple of weeks ago. There was an easiness about her.

She asked if I had come across her mother's birth document. She was doing the legal bits of the house inheritance and it wasn't vital to have the original record, but it would help speed up one little step.

I could imagine Malcolm: 'Don't let her have anything. Let her wait. Keep things from her.'

I said that I would get things to her later in the day. If Malcolm was going to give me responsibility for things, then I was sure going to exercise my version of being responsible.

It felt as if she needed to talk – as if the whole email/ meeting/ coffee/ birth document thing were merely a pretext to have a conversation with some other human being.

I can't recall her exact conversation – monologue, really, as I hardly said anything – but something like:

'We weren't close, my mother and I, as you may have gathered. None of that was her fault. All down to me, to be honest. Yet she was my mother; always there in the background ... in reserve, as needed. To be taken as needed, like some medicine.

But then – at the funeral – it hit me: There was no-one there anymore.

I have a nice apartment in downtown Toronto, but there is no-one there except me. It is empty. I come in to the echoes of when I was last there. There is only me in my life. Isn't that sad? I suppose it is a reflection of lots of things. Things might have been different, but that is where I ended up. Alone in a nice downtown apartment in one of the richest cities in the world. I'm not complaining. It is the life I have: The life I created for myself.

I was very close to Gran – Mother's Mom. She was a lovely person. Kind, understanding. Her arms were always open, and she had this particular smell that was unique to her.'

Why was she <u>telling</u> me all this? Why was she telling <u>me</u> all this?

'Mother died at a bad time for me.'

Tell you what, Margaret, I don't think it was the best time for her.

'I had all sorts of work pressures. I was due to retire in a couple of days' time. I was under pressure to tie everything up before I went. I was in functional, hit-the-deadline mode, then I got the call from Malcolm saying that Mother had died suddenly.

My first reaction – and I'm not proud of this – was to think "You inconsiderate old woman. Couldn't you wait until I had finished with all this retiring stuff?"

Is that terrible? Yes, I think it is. At best, I can say it was the shock, or the grief – but, when I am crying myself to sleep, alone in a fashionable apartment in Toronto, I have to be honest and admit that that is what I felt at the time. Does that make me a terrible person?'

I didn't answer.

'Dealing with the funeral felt like just one more task on my time-pressed To Do list. It was a project to be timed, costed, programmed, completed, got through, wrapped up.

The house feels like that. Most people would die to be left a house like that but to me it is a thing of my mother's, a thing to be managed, a thing to be got rid of. I certainly don't want to live in it. I was happy there a lot of the time. Even if Mother was erratic and a bit cranky. We lived with Gran. I know, now, that Mother was trying hard to do her best for me but to my teenage, probably arrogant – certainly selfish – self she was an embarrassment. I couldn't wait to get to university at the other side of the country.

I did get home fairly often, but the crunch came when I came home one Christmas and found a strange man sleeping in my bed. I stormed around, shouting, demanding, wanting to know Who the Hell? Why the Hell?

Mother refused to explain. She said that she couldn't explain, that it was important, and that maybe I could sleep on the couch in the living room. We had the row beyond all rows. I left and never saw the house as my home ever again.

It can't be my home now. There is way too much history in it. I will sell it. People are looking into that already. Developers are snapping up plots like that. Land value is currently higher than house value. The logic is to tear those old places down, free up the land, and put up something more appropriate to what city-dwellers of today need.'

Why do people tell me things? What do they want me to do with it?

Malcolm is celibate and regretful.

Margaret is retired and alone.

Elizabeth was gentle and now is dead.

These are disconnected facts. Reading them is like the slow intonation of some childhood primer:

The sun is red.

The ball is big.

Peter is a boy.

These tell you nothing, really. There is no narrative arc to engage with. You know no more at the end than you did at the beginning.

People come up to me in bars and start talking. It's a natural thing but they seem to talk to me more readily than normal and to open themselves up more easily. Why me: what is it about me that does that to people? Do I have some sort of confessional face?

*

Malcolm wants Elizabeth's rooms cleared. He has decided to rent them out. Why he is telling me, I don't know. The things in there are his by rights. Just because I took on one job as a favour, I got another, and another, and now he is telling me as if I am the one responsible for doing the clearing out.

He asks how I am getting on, but I don't think he really wants to know.

I have brought Elizabeth's notebooks, and some of her papers, back to my apartment to read in more detail.

Would Malcolm want to have them, really? He seems more concerned to hang on to the Elizabeth he knew rather than delve into sides of her she didn't want people to know about. He doesn't seem like the kind of person who wants his images challenged or shattered. He is a quiet-life guy.

If I gave him anything he might give it a quick glance, then throw it away. I can't see him hanging on to it.

To me, on the other hand, things from Elizabeth's past are full of possibilities.

They might trigger ideas, throw up potential storylines but, more than that, they are of interest simply because they were Elizabeth's.

Maybe the notebooks are of more use to me than to either Malcolm or Margaret. Neither of them had claimed them when they had the chance.

Maybe I will just keep what I want.

Elizabeth has got herself into my head.

I want to know lots more about her. I want to piece her back together again and know her in ways that Malcolm, and maybe even Margaret, never did.

*

Getting on the SkyTrain at Granville there was this little cameo of Canadian politeness – a real-life enactment of the self-deprecating joke about two Canadians insisting, 'After you'/'No, after you' so that no-one ever moves. They almost let the train go before they hopped on. Is this some inner truth about us as a nation – polite, not letting anything happen?

I am Canadian, but what does that mean?

Canadian by parentage? (Except mine were English heritage on Dad's side and Scottish on Mom's side. Most Canadians are historically out of somewhere else – except First Nations, and even they were Siberian incomers at some stage).

Canadian by place of birth? (Me as the outcome of some lottery based on lines on a map?)

Canadian by sentiment or loyalty? (I know the words of O Canada; I warm to the Maple Leaf design).

Canadian by choice? (I had absolutely no say in the matter).

People put such store by it. Politicians play on it. But does it really matter?

Nationality: Canadian, is the one thing binding us all in this minidrama - Elizabeth, Margaret, Malcolm, me. I'm not sure about Raphael, although I am never sure about anything with him.

When I am in New York I am still a Canadian. It is part of who I am. Here, I definitely am Canadian, through and through.

There was one time, recently, when I was taken for American. I was in a bar on Davie and this scary-tattoo girl came and sat next to me at the bar. I say 'girl' only because I am not sure she was even sixteen. She wanted small talk. I told her I lived in New York, which set her off on a rant: 'That president of yours …. that Mr T …. that pumpkin-head macho motormouth ….' She went off on a stream that didn't end when her head drooped down onto her arm on the bar counter. There was this mound of hair, this tattooed neck, and this grinding mumbling monotone. I left. I suspect that if I had gone back an hour later she would still be there, mumbling to herself. She will stay with me for a while, a character in so many ways.

*

Article in today's Metro paper about the possibility of reconstituting mammoths from bits of unearthed DNA.

What if the possibilities were there to reconstitute people from traces of their genetic material: Elizabeth brought back to life from bits of her left on her brushes and canvases – to confront Margaret? To tell things to Malcolm that she didn't have time to say before she died? To enliven herself through a refreshed sense of artistry?

My own parents brought back from traces of their handprints on books I have? What would I say to them; and what would they say to me after all this time?

Would I want myself reconstituted? – and that raises all sorts of philosophical questions about what counts as 'self'.

Would anyone want to bring back the past, even if it were scientifically possible? Would they really want to have to live things all over again?

*

Wills are the basis of so much fiction. People angered or frustrated by the decisions of the deceased:

- Not getting the thing most coveted, and still coveting it.
- Unexpectedly, and to the chagrin of others, being left something of great value.
- Being publicly rebuked: '…and to my husband I leave twenty dollars with the proviso that it be spent on even more wine.'
- Controlling the lives of those left behind through what gets written at time of death.
- Houses left to indolent pet cats. Money given to unworthy charities.
- Long-lost relatives and children the family don't know about are wheeled onto the stage.

- The family gather to pick over the left-behinds. What goes on in the circling round, the not wanting to be first to dive onto the broach or the tiny speck of treasure?
- Then there are the burdens handed down. The talisman that becomes an albatross. The amulet with the power to change the lives of those cursed to wear it.

Dramas get played out.

The dead lumber us with themselves. Even though they are no longer there to watch over us, they trouble us with what to do with their belongings.

When does it all become nothing more than accumulated rubbish, kept alive by the feelings absorbed into its fabric? Are we inheriting things or emotions? Can we get rid of them until we have purged ourselves of those emotional ties? Emotions are hard things to slough off.

*

Workmen have uncovered a ghost-sign during work to renovate a 'boutique grocery store' (Boutique: It's a grocery store, for goodness sake!). One wall had wooden panelling over plaster. When this was removed, the plaster crumbled, and underneath was a sign saying BUSINESS OFFICE - for a long-defunct Vancouver Daily World newspaper.

Worlds get covered over, buried under plaster and wood, only to unexpectedly reveal themselves later: history emerging by peeling off the present. Horizontal archaeology. Universes layered upon universes – layers of an onion.

In New York I often see fading signs high up on the sides of buildings - clues of former businesses that once operated there – legacies of a past that has moved on, meaningless to passing commuters.

I checked out that word that had kept coming and going in my mind: Palimpsest.

To do with writing being scraped off to reveal a clean surface that gets written on again, so that traces of the past get layered upon each other – pasts stacking up; pasts being stripped back.

*

I may be getting in a rut, which isn't the same as being on track. Each day: Two different free newspapers, then buy a copy of the Vancouver Sun and head for a coffee; notebook handy; brain engaged (after the coffee if not before); laptop on; eyes scanning the others around me. If it were wartime I might make a passable spy. As it is, here in the peace of Vancouver (well, peaceful for me. I suspect there are many in the city for whom daily life is far from peaceful), the best I can offer is to aspire to get some random jottings on the page.

Nothing in the papers. In desperation I glanced at my horoscope – something I normally never do.

LIBRA (Sep 23 – Oct 22).

The full moon mid-month will shine on those things that need your full attention. Things need decisive action from you. You are well-known for indecisiveness but now is the time to step forward and be bold. Watch for over-reaching yourself though. Watch out for over-doing things. Jupiter's benign influence will help you see the big picture. Now is your time. Now is your destiny.

This was a far cry from the usual wishy-washy blandness. I felt personally spoken to.

Even so, planets exerting some distant influence on my fate through celestial imaginations of dot-to-dot drawings that could be scales or scorpions or a crab: Unlikely.

Think I might invent a whole alternative system. If Trump can build so much out of the idea of Alternative Facts, then I can come up with some better alternative than being on the cusp of Libra and Scorpio.

*

Crime/detective stories are topping the best-seller list. I don't see myself as a best-seller writer (A writer for interest? A not-sure-why-I-do-it writer?) but maybe I should have a go at writing a detective tale. Not one of those postmodern psychological twisting and turning stories. Not one of those closed-house Agatha Christie stories where anyone could have done it and the detective calls everyone into the Library to dramatically reveal whodunnit. And not one of those CSI high-tech things.

I would opt for a traditional tale based on New York; an old-time cop; a puzzle to be pieced together by straight observation.

It will hinge on him having a past.

Maybe he gets called to a body on a vacant lot. He checks things over. He knows people from his days as a rookie cop on the beat. One couple has an apartment overlooking the lot and tell him what they saw. He pieces things together. Maybe he comes to the conclusion that the killer had to be someone he knows, someone he works with. He can't prove it, though. He has to live with the possibility that one of his colleagues is a killer.

I'll give it a shot.

*

Change of tune from Malcolm. He does blow with the wind.

The Korean couple are not coming back. Something to do with staying on to look after relatives and sort out some family business. Their apartment is being emptied by a friend. Elizabeth has gone, and he wants her stuff cleared. To seal everything, it appears that Raphael has moved out – for good this time, not one of his temporary trips away.

'Had to happen one day. Better for both of us. We were too on top of each other, emotionally.'

I will be going back to New York at some stage soon, so the whole place is emptying around him.

He says that he has had enough. He has contacted his brother, who wants to sell up and turn his asset into cash. The whole block will be going up for sale. The realty agent visited earlier today and, according to Malcolm, talked of things being a bit run down, a bit old-fashioned, needing a bit of a make-over. 'Not sure if he was talking about the block or about me,'

*

Malcolm suddenly wants to see Elizabeth's paintings and other stuff. I had no other commitments.

I spread the documents on the work-surface in the kitchen area. Some things were draped over the edge of the chest. The paintings took a bit of sorting.

Some of the canvases were unfinished or were simplified sketches for later paintings. Some had been partly washed over in white. (Elizabeth's version of crossing out pieces she felt were mistakes?) The twenty others were lined up resting against the trestle table.

Malcolm (as I had suspected) scanned the documents with little enthusiasm; asked me if the letters said anything of interest – but didn't wait for a reply before moving to the paintings.

'As you know, Donald, I am no expert on anything artistic. I did, many years ago, do a part-time Art History course but that doesn't mean I know if these paintings are any good.'

At the same time, I could see his eyes sweeping backwards and forwards across each work, trying hard to guess at the value.

I think he had switched from the Malcolm directly after the funeral (These paintings are Elizabeth's. They carry too much of her. They radiate emotion. I can't handle that.) to the Malcolm scanning around (These paintings are mine now. They hold some potential. If I handle them well, they may bring recognition for Elizabeth as an overlooked artist of merit. That would be a good memorial; something I can do for her. It might mean that the works become valuable).

I may be doing him wrong, but it feels that Elizabeth as a person, as a friend, had gone – replaced by Elizabeth as an abstraction, or an investment.

Can that happen so easily?

I wondered what it had cost Elizabeth – personally and financially - to hold off on her early experiences with other artists. She had taken on various jobs. She had raised Margaret, with the help of her mother Agnes. She had cared for Agnes for around twenty years. What does twenty years of caring do to a person? When does love slide into resentment (even hatred)?

Somewhere in all of that she found a way back to art. She was a determined soul.

I think Malcolm read my mind.

'She didn't have an easy life, Donald. Things were a struggle for her. We became good friends. It was clear that she had creativity that had been held back. It seemed that she had things in her that wanted to come out. I bought her canvases and paints. It seemed the least I could do. She resisted at first but saw the sense eventually. The apartment became vacant around the same time and when I showed it to her she was knocked out by the space, the open view, but mostly by the light. She was so in love with the space that I just offered it as a studio. It meant a drop in rental income, but I could afford it. "You can pay me back when you are rich and famous," I used to say to her.'

I know that his brother does all the interfacing with City Hall and the revenue people so maybe Elizabeth's studio got put down as some form of tax break. Even so it was kind of Malcolm to do that for Elizabeth.

I reminded him that the paintings were his now and that he needed a plan for them – a plan based on the value of Elizabeth's work: financially and artistically.

*

People move through life leaving trails behind them. If we were snails you would see where we had been, the slimy remnants of our laboured movements. Each point in that trail would fix where we had been, where we had come from, what we had achieved so far. It would set our past in stone (or in slime on stone). The past is all that there is at that point.

The same point holds all the potential of what we might be, where we might go, what might happen to us – but the past is all there is. The sudden crunching boot, the pecking bird, the mate eager to writhe momentarily across our body – all those future possibilities do not exist, yet.

The past is all there is of us. We are the sum of past actions, decisions, events. We move on, leaving a wake. We career forward, leaving paths not chosen, jobs not taken, loves and lives abandoned. We move through the world leaving traces behind us – the bits of us that have rubbed off, the air we have huffed and puffed in anger or ecstasy, the tears that have dribbled from us.

There is that thing about every breath we take containing at least one atom from Einstein – or some other notable we wouldn't mind having inside us, ready to be incorporated into our feebleness. The example never includes the possibilities of the atoms being from Hitler, or Stalin, or Pol Pot. Nor do we usually claim the reverse – that some bit of Obama, or Kennedy, or Trudeau, is really a few atoms of us. We make them what they are.

People move on, unpredictably, through life. What are the chances of two paths crossing?

Could I have unknowingly stumbled across the lives of any of the others who take up so much of my time now – Malcolm? Elizabeth? Margaret? Even Raphael? Could I have passed them in a street somewhere, or sat next to them in the subway – breathing their atoms into me, rubbing bits of me off onto them?

Unlikely. Malcolm shifted from Edmonton to Vancouver and I shifted from Vancouver to Edmonton, but not in ways that meant our paths would have crossed.

With Elizabeth and Margaret, the maths and the geography are against it. We were all in Vancouver in 1972. I was a baby. Margaret was coming home from university, briefly, to find some unknown man in her bed. Elizabeth was here in the West End, looking after the ailing Agnes whilst I toddled in a restricted world on a street overlooking False Creek.

The house is still there. I went to find it the other day – out of what: Nostalgia? Curiosity? A sense of rootlessness? Today it has a clear-air view over the water and the development constructed for the Olympic Games. Then, at least in my mind and probably in reality, it was a dusty place with a view over factories, the remnants of industry – and smoke (I remember the smell of smoke when the wind was in a certain direction – but it may all be false memories of a past False Creek).

Elizabeth may have visited the bakery at the corner of our street but that would be a fair trek just for some bread. Dad may have taken me to city-centre shops, but I have no memories of that. I have no reliable memories of those early years in Vancouver, just some emotional triggers triangulated around Home – Hospital – Bakery.

A young guy in a bar, trying to make conversation, just to be polite:

What did I think of the upcoming elections?

His view: There wasn't anything to get excited about, nothing to make you shout "Hell. Yeah". There were the same old slogans; permutations on a few catchy words.

This year it was Strong Province: Brighter Future.

Vote for us and we'll make everything great again.

People don't, in his opinion, want promises. They have been promised the moon and back in the past. None of it has been real. They want some reality. Someone to tell life as it is for most people.

People were already sick of soundbites and photo-ops: Politician flipping pancakes; politician driving a bulldozer.

He didn't like the way politicians were too quick to point the finger; were too busy sparring to say what they might actually get done.

He thought that they all lie. They just make stuff up.

He went on about pipelines, about natural gas and big business corrupting the election.

He went on about the Liberals and NDP being neck and neck, letting the Greens or the handful of Conservatives have too much leverage on things.

He went on about various groups favouring various parties – Korean Liberals, Filipino New Democrats – Something he had read in the paper.

He went on about the census showing that grey-haired Canadians now outstripped the young, and how that was keeping things as they were.

Generally, though, he just went on ….. and on …. and on.

I don't know how many more think like him. I have even less idea how the few people I know intend to vote.

Malcolm: I don't see him lining up to legalize pot or to raise welfare levels, but I can see him (if only out of self-interest) supporting subsidies to renters and lobbying for improved city transit. On balance, I have him as a wavering Liberal.

Maybe he is more committed than I give him credit for.

Maybe his vote can be taken for granted by some party, releasing them to ignore him and put all their attention onto the Undecideds?

Is the outcome down to who can best swing a handful of people in a handful of ridings?

Some newswoman the other day was quoting analysis in the US which suggested that if a few thousand people in a tiny number of voting places had gone otherwise then it would have been "Good morning, Madam President".

And you, Elizabeth, where did your allegiances lie, I wonder?

*

The library readings on psychogeography have been interesting – all those new words added to my collection.

The random wanderings, picking up on what is stumbled across; the semi-conscious going with the emotional tugs of things; the deliberate exploration of abandoned spaces.

I have my own daily meanderings. No exact pattern, but I do walk the same streets. I do roughly the same things, for no particular reason. What if there was a reason? What would drive me to repeat and repeat, day after day, compulsively?

I knocked ideas around whilst walking and came up with some outline fiction.

Someone could have a daily ritual of walking the streets of New York, but not in some aimless way. He walks and walks, the same route, over and over – wearing away at the pavements; inscribing a message that only he knows (but which someone following the story, with a map of the city to hand, could interpret).

Maybe having him tell his story to some random stranger sitting next to him – one of those things about paths arbitrarily crossing; information being exchanged in casual conversation – to have effect or to be forgotten.

Something along the lines of:

There are times when I need to let the thing overflow onto someone else, if only to prevent it consuming me altogether. For now, you will do nicely. There is no-one else.

People sometime believe what I say; they sometime discount me. I know it is true and that is all that matters; that and occasionally reducing the pressure in my head.

I am telling you no more than I tell the others. That I have a route. That there are things I do because I must. That New York streets are the key to it all. That if you could only rise above the city itself, looking down on the huddled masses, then you might glimpse what it is all about.

I weave a pattern onto New York's own, over and again to hold everything in place. To stop it all unravelling. I don't want it sliding away. I want to hold on to it. It is all I have got.

The city has reshaped itself. Not just physically, but psychologically. It has gone from manufacturing to tourism; production to consumption.

Vancouver will change again, that is for sure. Maybe it will mostly be a place of craft beers, shaped beards, miniparks and festivals, green walkways with public art. A place of selfies and entertainment.

Its economy may be based on filmings, on gamings, on digital money made and spent – things circulating amongst the same groups. Gated communities – middle-income gang areas - even where those gates are invisible boundaries in the mind: symbols and subtleties; unseen Do Not Cross policing of areas. Homeless people knowing their place – held in other areas, in holding pens with supervised drug use, legalised sales, soup cafes – social leper colonies – with separations from the creative quarters. New Creatives populating creative colonies, not in cold cabins by the water's edge but in contemporary waterfront homes. Their boundless creativity held in an echo chamber.

I came across a neat huge pendulum swinging in the foyer of a bank on West Georgia. Strange thing was that I had been told about it, searched it out and then stood looking around not seeing it – whilst all the while it was there, enormous, arcing across the whole space. How can you look for something and not be able to see it because it is too obvious?

*

Elizabeth's newspaper cuttings were from the late 1950s to 1992. Vancouver Sun mostly. During this period did she read the paper daily? It feels as if she did.

She had some clear reason to tear out particular pages and keep them:

- An obituary for a longstanding resident of West End. The surname, Brown, wasn't anything to do with Agnes, so far as I know. Maybe one of her neighbour friends. If I bump into any of the ones from the funeral I could ask them.
- Articles on draft dodgers coming over the border. Raids on city homes. People moving people along forest trails to little-visited villages and on into the depths of the country.

- Several articles on the clearing of something called the Jungle.
- An article on changes in Aboriginal Art. It talked of changes from a time when Native Art was criminalised; then recognised; then, as First Nation people went through studies at art schools, it was influenced by other ideas around those days. So, it asked, what is an original, authentic culture?
- An article on a scandal: A Vancouver art group had been allocated Federal funding before it had even been established. Headline: 'Non-Existent Arts Organisation receives Government Funds'
- An article on What Counts as Vancouver Canadian Art.
- An article on artists who were into experimentation, drugs, freedoms and so on. They followed Californian West Coast ideals. There was a rejection of galleries and the other trappings of the art institutions. The streets were the new canvas. There was performance art mixed with psychedelic music concerts, mixed with experimental film, mixed with anything else going. Everything was fragmented. Squatters and Hippies were the new avant-garde.
- A review about art and the city. City blocks being sold and razed to make way for the new

capitalism. Artist colonies and squattings being burned down; artists moving out to the next neighbourhood. As old areas were knocked down, the city was seen as being on the road to ruin. Vancouver was losing its soul. Vancouver itself – the nature of the city – became the subject matter for artists. The old got photographed and collaged onto the new.

*

An email today from the caretaker of the apartment block in New York giving all tenants a bit of a heads up. He has been told by the landlord that the owners of the block are selling out to a finance investment group. They own other plots in the neighbourhood and are putting forward some Grand Plan that involves upping the status of our block, which will almost certainly involve upping the rent levels.

Jerry from #609 replied round everyone. He has gone through the rental agreement for our block and there it was in the small print: The landlord is an agent for some finance group ('shady' finance group in Jerry's terms, but then he does see everything from that sort of perspective); there is a clause about alternative accommodation being offered in the event of .. blah, blah – lot of legalese.

None of us had paid much attention because it all read as if they would be helpful to tenants if things went wrong. It could be interpreted differently. Jerry had phoned the landlord and, yes, the block renovation was going to be more extensive than at first. It would take a lot longer, be 'comprehensive', with the offer of apartments in another block at the far end of Queens. Meanwhile the finance company – 'General Universal Money Machine' in Jerry's language – would be sending out new Agreements at new levels of rent.

*

It seems fairly clear who currently owns the canvases. Elizabeth bequeathed them to Malcolm.

When he was moving them to his apartment he asked me to choose one to keep for myself, 'in recognition of all that I had done for him and dear Elizabeth'.

I have kept one of the mid-size ones: a mass of swirling blues, greys and greens. There is something vital about it – something organic (visceral, even). It is the only one I like, to be honest, but I really do like it.

I sit looking at it as the sun starts to go down mid-evening. The shapes seem to pick up shadows, the colours change tone – the meaning seems to change.

It goes from a sense of resignation in the face of an overwhelming nature (ocean/forest etc) to a sense of optimism as the textures open up. The hope of the urban. I am no art-lover or art-expert, but I really love the effect it has.

What makes a painting valuable (and does Elizabeth's work have any value)? Does recognition come through exhibiting, through sales, through coverage in art columns, through being included in the permanent collection of some gallery or other?

She was obviously part of some group but never felt herself to be a key member. She gave up on painting to be a mother, a daughter, a widow, a carer, a person always caring and worrying about others. At the same time, when the opportunity opened up again, via Malcolm, she jumped right back in.

She has produced work but not had an exhibition. She went to other people's exhibitions, on and off. She has the fading catalogues to show for it. She kept art-related cuttings from the local newspapers. She kept the link, whatever else was happening in her life. She was determined to be an artist – recognised or not.

Malcolm did what he could to make this happen.

*

I feel a bit sorry for Vancouver – coming from New York as I do. Both have their grand Park; both have sea walkways and sea views. Vancouver has its main art gallery, a good contemporary one and a scattering of interesting others; but New York has MOMA, the Met, the Guggenheim, the streets of local galleries out by the High Line. Need I go on?

In those galleries I can look at the whole of US, and other, art – all those iconic Pollocks, Hoppers, Warhols … all there is in art that counts.

In Vancouver Art Gallery I can look at the Group of Seven and a bit of other stuff.

The Group of Seven: everyone learns about them in school. The curriculum then tends to shift to the well-known international artists. I know little about later Canadian artists - ones from the 1950s to now. It is as if they didn't really exist outside of a closed art world.

Was there an artist Colony in Vancouver (One that Elizabeth was part of)? How would I find out?

Maybe Elizabeth was no Emily Carr, but Canada maybe has only room for one Emily Carr.

*

Elizabeth's faded arts catalogues and magazines:

A copy of 1949 'Art News'. The page corner was turned down at a feature on a leading avant-garde artist in Vancouver; a key name in Canadian modernist art. He never featured in my art lessons at school.

Several other magazines, mostly with pages turned down.

Various catalogues for exhibitions in Vancouver. More than half were for women artists – sculpture, photography, abstracts, figurative paintings, constructions using found objects ….

So, it is not that there were no recognised women artists, nor that there were no exhibitions by women artists, it was just that Elizabeth wasn't one of them.

Maybe she aspired, hoped, yearned, wanted. Maybe she tried, resigned, gave up – although that doesn't sound like the Elizabeth that comes through her other stuff.

Maybe there could be hope yet for Elizabeth.

Is that Malcolm's new mission? After trying to save Raphael from himself, does he move on to resurrect Elizabeth?

He will never shake off church-thinking. It is built into his bones.

*

A few months ago, I hardly thought about issues that didn't directly affect me. I rarely paid much attention to housing policies, house prices, real estate legislation, and so on. I could scan a newspaper and skate over such articles.

Now, I have got myself embroiled (or rather been embroiled by my landlord) in what is to be done with one particular house in Vancouver. Emails from back home are focused on what is happening at my, or rather some finance company's, apartment block in New York.

Housing is suddenly on my radar, all compounded by homeless people asking for cash by day or noisily diving into my garbage bins by night.

In just the last couple of days, stuff has leapt out:

- The price of the average detached house in the Greater Toronto area has shot up by 33% over the last twelve months … and has been rising for years ('like an infection, a disease').
- Greater Toronto Area has grown by nearly 400,000 people in the past five years and MetroVancouver has grown by nearly 150,000 people – driving a need for more housing …
- More homes are being built but it never seems enough. Homes sell in a week, sending prices out of whack …

- To stop foreign investors buying apartments in Vancouver and leaving them empty, British Columbia tries a foreign buyers tax.
- Landlords can jack up rents if they can show that market conditions have changed in the neighbourhood. One newspaper talks of 'renovictions' and 'demovictions' – not heard these phrases before.
- A social housing block has been taken over by new managers, who are very religious. Now the whole block is being turned dry, non-smoking, clear of pets, notices forbidding yelling or advertising bible study sessions. Cultural cleansing?

*

I bumped into one of the neighbours from the funeral. It doesn't feel as if that was almost a couple of months ago. There have been several weeks of me wandering in the neighbourhood with no sighting of any of Elizabeth's neighbour friends until now. People really can hide themselves away. I went into the corner coffee shop and there she was, waving me over to her table.

I asked her what Elizabeth's family had been like.

It turns out that Agnes was the strong driving force. It was she who pushed the family into moving from Poland in the first place. I had assumed that the husband had moved for work but (shouldn't make assumptions) it was Agnes's compassion that had triggered the change.

She was someone who always wanted other people's lives to be better. She would give you her last dollar if she thought it would help – but was no easy touch. The fact that she was strong-minded and strong-willed kept coming up ('She had no time for people who didn't want to try. Did I already tell you that?')

Agnes, according to this coffee-sipping neighbour, was sensitive, temperamental and kind all at the same time.

Her strong-mindedness had rubbed off on Elizabeth, apparently.

I asked about the husband: Elizabeth's father. In return I got an impersonation of a gruff voice: 'You dragged us across continents and oceans, and for what? For the rain? We had rain enough already in Poland.' I could immediately feel the guy's coldness and frustrations.

'.. and yet,' the neighbour, between sips, 'and yet he read a lot, went to talks, could hold his own on any topic. You just got the sense that he would rather be doing it back home, not in some rain-soaked foreign city.'

She knew Elizabeth as a girl. In Germany. The neighbour (I really must ask her name if we bump into each other again) lived in the town that Agnes dragged her family to – 'almost next door, near neighbours then like now.'

Elizabeth moved on to England and the neighbour moved on to Canada. The families had stayed in touch which was how they all ended up in the West End of Vancouver, years later.

The two girls played in each other's houses in Germany. They made puppets and put on little shows. When they were due to go separate ways, each girl made a little doll out of scraps of material and exchanged them, keepsakes, with the promise that the two dolls would see each other again sometime.

The two girls met again as teenagers. They were still friends but never recaptured the bond they had had as girls.

When Elizabeth left home, the neighbour provided an informal route for information to get back to Elizabeth's mother.

They had stayed in touch ever since.

'It's a long story,' she said, 'but then most interesting stories need a certain length to tell them properly.'

Agnes did various jobs. She spent a lot of time making clothes for local stores. In her spare time, she helped out in welfare work with street women in the

West End. I must have looked surprised. This quiet area was once a hotbed of street vice, apparently.

'There is a memorial lamp-post somewhere near the church over there,' she waved vaguely, and held her coffee cup out for a top-up.

*

The Museum here has information about how Vancouver treated its enemy-citizens in the Second World War. The Japanese were treated badly it seems. They had their property taken from them to pay for board and lodgings in an inland camp. These weren't luxurious affairs. Some were cheap-build bungalow houses that were constructed on stilts if the area was swampy.

The people were given an alternative to internment in these camps and that was, even if they were Canadian by birth, to be relocated to Japan. To me it whiffs of the way things are today. 'Build a camp. Make them pay for it. Otherwise send them home'. It probably made sense to some nationally-minded Canadians at the time but must have destroyed lives and livelihoods.

I also hadn't known that, even in the First World War, Canada had internment and concentration camps. The start of World War 1 led to arrest and internment of foreign nationals – Ukrainians, Germans, Austrians – more than 8,000 men scattered to 24 concentration camps across the country.

A 1917 report said prisoners were destitute, beaten and bullied. Canada misapplied the International Convention, illegally using non-military POWs as labour for building roads – paying 55 cents a day but taking back 30 cents of that for room and board at the camp.

Why did I not know about this? One reason was that much of the information was destroyed by the government because there was no room to store it. At least, that is their story.

I have lived almost all my life in a glorious country, whose history I studied at school, which had secret histories, hidden histories – things not mentioned in the politeness that was built into the essence of Canada.

*

What else was in the trunk?

Baby boots and cloak.

Could be the basis for a short story?

Hemingway wrote a story in 6 words. Something like "For Sale: baby shoes, never worn". Amazing to be able to capture a huge set of emotions in just six words.

It got me thinking about six-word sentences – but none were anywhere near Hemingway class. I did get a few starting points for possible storylines:

Future System wins, despite girl's efforts.

Set in 2097. Main protagonist is a teenage girl, which will provide me with some challenges.

Issues – Can a forty-year-old male write as if he were a teenage girl? Can a man legitimately write from the perspective of a woman? There is so much written about Cultural Appropriation these days that you are frightened to write as anything but yourself – so everything becomes endless autobiography in thin disguise.

Cecil Centaur discovers his dark side

We have had vampires, zombies, sparkly unicorns – so what is the next big thing? What should I start on now if I am to create a wave? Mermaids? Centaurs??

*

There is a quirky bookshop just off the city centre. It isn't easy to find. It is more stumbled across than headed to. The whole shop is designed for exploration, for coming upon interesting things, for sudden excitements. There are piles of books in corners, stacked at odd angles.

It is like an old library I go to in New York. I spend hours rambling between shelves. The librarian fits the place: Half-rim glasses, hair in a bun, grey cardigan pulled round and partially buttoned, nose ring and tiny tattoo. Both expected and unexpected at the same time.

The shop has textbooks, full of theorisations, and popular books, full of historical snapshots of the man with a railway spike through his head, the man who couldn't recognise his wife…. People with all sorts of acronymic conditions: ADHD, OCD, or autism – Illnesses? Conditions? Stretches of normality or something so different that can only be seen as abnormal?

It is a source of cheap books on psychology.

How minds work fascinates me.

There are people who have described having several films running at once in their head, anticipating what is going to happen (and get anxious when real life doesn't follow the script). They rerun films of what has just happened and worry if they feel things were wrong. For them it is about synchronisation and life getting out-of-synch.

There are others with voices in their head. Not necessarily multiple personalities – just an endless cacophony. Their days are psychedelic soundscapes. What must that be like? How do they live with that?

Or there is the whole thing of people sensing things in multiple ways – numbers have colour, as do sounds, and so on.

There are so many writing-triggers from those books.

A starting point is to write brief cameos of quirky characters, not attempting an ongoing storyline, just getting a brief glimpse inside their head.

I have invented a new writing technique.

When I go for my morning coffee I take a single sheet of paper. Scanning through the day's papers I usually find some picture of an interesting-looking face. It may be of someone famous, but I ignore that. All I want is the face. Or I might watch the other customers. Not the ones in the line-up waiting for coffee-to-go, but the ones sitting for long enough to let their face fill my brain.

I imagine them a personality to go with that face, and I give that personality some quirk.

It may be synaesthesia, or face-blindness, or some unique form of repetitive behaviour.

The writing challenge is to tell their tale, starting at the top left corner and ending exactly at the bottom right of the page – a personality captured in a few hundred words.

*

I caught the end of a local news program on the disappearing city.

Tens of thousands of demolitions have already happened or are scheduled. Buildings, sometimes whole blocks, are disappearing. The city is losing some things and gaining other, different things.

What is worth preserving?

Everything, just because it is old? The past can't be clung on to forever. Space has to be made for the needs of today.

Cases can be made to preserve things that connect to the history of Vancouver, at least to its rich and famous. Some of their homes had state-of-the-art craftsmanship and only the best wood. In some houses the timber alone is worth a quarter of a million in today's money. Rip it out; start all over. Why have someone else's best when the city can have a more modern best of everything?

There was a bit about the West End. My mind focused.

Initially, the area was desirable for richer families. It was all part of the early century property boom that made fortunes for some developers.

After the Great War, the large draughty houses got partitioned off as cheaper rooming houses, or converted into hospitals or private schools.

The grand houses had belonged to a past world. Their reasons for being had gone. The sugar, timber and liquor magnates took their families to more desirable streets in Shaughnessy or Point Grey.

The residual West End population shifted into multi-occupied lodgings, and the area took on a red-light seediness.

There was a discussion on the changing house market.

One city home had been bought and sold by various families, for tens of thousands of dollars. More recently it changed hands for more than a million dollars. It has stood empty for more than a decade, and now it is for sale at more than $7million, with planning permission to knock it down and build a contemporary luxury home on the site.

This has pushed house prices way beyond what was reasonable. It has left apartments empty whilst Canadian citizens are being made homeless.

Inevitably, in the program's phone-in, someone pointed out that being a resident who was being squeezed out by incoming people from abroad was exactly what the First Nation people had experienced for more than a hundred years.

Views and counter views were put.

The program settled for keeping some stuff but always being vibrant, always developing.

The problem I had with the whole debate was that each point made seemed obviously true, only for the next (and opposing) view to seem equally valid. I can be swayed back and forward until I will almost believe anything.

*

There has been no sign of Malcolm for a few days.

No billet-doux, no meeting at the elevator, no hesitant tapping on my door, no raised voices from beyond his door.

I hope he hasn't gone off looking for Raphael – or gone off on some jaunt, trying to be Raphael. There is probably some simple explanation.

I asked Sam. He reassured me that Malcolm had been at home every night but had been busy with something or other during the day: 'Some bit of business that needs tidying up,' Malcolm had told him.

I knocked on his door – lightly; briskly; tentatively; in a business-like manner. I tried several styles of knockings, at different times of the day. One runs out of adverbs with which to attack a door.

Whatever the style of knocking, it was all the same: No reply.

*

People get labelled and the label becomes them (or they become the label). People become seen only as Senator, Premier, Chief Executive, Head of IT, and so on.

At the same time people are fragments held loosely together. If the fragments hang together securely and with some coherence, then they come across as authentic, unified etc.. If the fragments are more tentatively connected, the jaggedness shows through.

At one time I was a combination of son, grandson, student, lover, tenant, ….

At another time I was tenant, bar worker, explorer of New York, ….

Now I am explorer of Elizabeth, intermediary for Malcolm, researcher of quirky things, jotter of everyday puzzles, and someone who should be writing far more than I am.

*

Grandad Donald would have loved what is going on in his own country these days. I only get the version filtered through the Canadian press. I suppose I could watch BBC News, but I don't.

The UK population were offered a Referendum on leaving Europe which really meant leaving the constraints of rules and regulations imposed by membership of the European Union.

A whole range of complexities were bundled up by politicians into simple slogans. 'Take back control of our borders'; 'British laws via British courts' and so on – all versions of 'Make This Country Great Again'.

In areas where EU workers had come to Britain, the referendum was seen in terms of preventing 'the flow of foreigners'.

Others saw it as getting rid of restrictive bureaucracy. 'Restore Our Fishing Fleet' by getting rid of EU quotas. Or about magically restoring lost industries.

For others it was about money. Campaign vehicles carried painted slogans saying 'Funds paid to Europe should be kept to finance health services here'.

The Referendum itself offered simply Stay In or Get Out as the options. Everyone had a different view of what this meant. No wonder the split vote left the country confused about what had just been voted for.

Grandad would have got to the end of it all. He would have written it up in ways for people to understand. He would have helped clarify without over-simplifying.

In his day, being a writer was a calling, a vocation.

In his day, there were properly employed reporters. They spent time learning a craft, being edited and sub-edited. They spent time on the words. They hit deadlines. They took pride. Now it is trending towards citizen journalism; reader involvement ('Your News', 'Your Photos').

Once it was writing for people.

Now it is people writing.

Anyone can knock out a Word document, publish as an ebook and call themselves a writer. Anyone can write blogs, do podcasts and hope to become famous. The driver may be money, or the driver may be celebrity. For me, the driver is wanting to prove something. I don't know what that is, but it is connected back to Grandad being a newspaper man – a writer.

For me, it's simply all about being a writer.

I took Elizabeth's old box of jewellery into an antique shop. The answer was quick. The jewels were worthless. They were good, someone had produced them with care, but were of no real monetary value. The kind of thing one might wear to create an impression of something else: A front; a pretence.

The box, on the other hand, was of great interest.

The guy was guessing, he said, but his view would be: Mid-Eighteenth Century; Eastern European; high quality craftsmanship ('superb' was the word he used) in best quality wood; inlaid with silver.

To the right person, in the right auction, it would be worth a lot of money.

So, a classic case of Figure and Ground – so busy looking at the one thing (the jewels) that the other (the box) was not seen. Value hiding in plain sight. Something shouting out but only to the ones prepared to hear its message. To others, distracted by the dazzles, it was merely a container.

*

I read recently about how our idea of memory has changed. It used to be thought that memories were stored, each in its separate box. Pigeon-holed, a huge warehouse full of evidence boxes all labelled and filed, and some old half-forgotten guardian as the only one who remembers the somewhat idiosyncratic indexing system.

A 'lost' memory is then a box not put back in the right place with the possibility of it being stumbled upon surprisingly, having slipped down behind other boxes. Open the lid and there is the whole memory readily back in place.

The current view is more complicated. Each time it is called to mind, a memory has to be reconstructed from fragments stored in distributed form across the brain. It is a wonder, on this model, that more memories aren't reconstructed differently. It may be that links get broken and it becomes impossible to put that memory together in that specific way, even if the fragments are still there, itching to be constructed into something.

But how would we know? Each memory would feel that it is the right one, having no other memory to compare it to – we could end up living a life based on thousands of badly-constructed false memories.

*

Each city actively narrates its own future.

Who writes the city? What stories do people rely on to make sense of the city? What stories emanate from the planner, the artist, the resident, the casual visitor?

Cities are places of dreams and hopes and fears. They are open to debate and interpretation, with ambiguities around what is truth and what is fiction, what is real and what is unreal.

There may only ever be fragmented and fractured views of places, seen from different vantage points. There will always be invisibilities, things overlooked, unremarked details, secret folds and hidden corners.

The city is about flow and change and people and humanity. It is a sense that things are always just about to get out of control.

The city of today is arrived at through superimpositions, built up layer upon layer. Things waiting to be unearthed.

*

If we are individual bundles of unique memories of unique experiences, what about when we get dementia? What happens to our Self when those memory-underpinnings slip away? What if our mind's content could be transferred to another body? Which one would be our true Self: The old physical body with no mind, or the new different-looking body with all my memories intact?

How did Agnes become Agnes? Or Elizabeth become Elizabeth?

There was certainly a person that was uniquely Elizabeth, but can anyone ever really know who that person was?

In my imagination I had made her a woman whose last gasp was let out to blow across the cheek of the TV Trump.

In another imagined version of her, she is alive in the audience for a Canadian visit by Trump. She removes her shoe, uncomfortable in the high stiletto that is so out of character for her. She hurls the shoe and embeds the heel in that broad, flat forehead. Blood streams down, people scream and turn, security men close in on her. On investigation her true Self is revealed. She is a North Korean trained, Chinese-funded assassin with a superbly crafted backstory of Poland, Germany, Bolton, Vancouver, Colony … She is trapped in her own narrative. She is taken away for brainwashing to prise open her true identity.

*

I asked at the library if they had any old material on 1970s draft dodgers coming via Vancouver. They pointed me to an online report of a recent lecture at the Vancouver Historical Society.

The talk had covered a lot of detail: Thousands of draft resisters came to Canada – A mix of draft dodgers and actual deserters from the US army. Some were women wanting to support others in the anti-war activities, or to take their teenage sons out of reach of any potential future draft.

Vancouver was a centre of activity – a mix of Americans, local support networks and people opposed to the war in general. It was a focus for information about the best border crossing places, or places where border guards might be sympathetic. Women would move back and forth across the border taking messages between friends and families.

I started putting some pieces together.

How likely was it that Elizabeth was involved? The letter for appearance at court was from that time. The strange man in Margaret's bed, the one her mother wouldn't give any information about, was from that time.

I went over other bits and pieces; triangulating – coming up with something that was certainly not proof but was a serious likelihood.

*

Someone once asked me why my writings are like those Hopper paintings – solitary figures staring out into the distance or reflecting back on their own life. Maybe I should make the most of that. I have a stock of postcards of his work so maybe I should scatter all those Hopper mini-reproductions across the floor and arrange them in some storyboard, then get down to stringing a narrative together.

It has probably been done by someone already. It is too obvious not to have been.

Everything has probably been done before. Everything is a rehash from the same gene pool.

A story told from perspective of dead victim? Done before.

A story told from perspective of about-to-be-born child? Just been done.

Even if it has been done, do I still write in the way Hopper painted? If so, my style is Bleak, Urban, Mysterious. Is that my elevator pitch? Doesn't sound overly attractive. In fact, it sounds old-fashioned, twenty years out of time.

Maybe that is what I am: A Man Out of Time. At least that sounds a promising title – although even that has probably been used before (Note to self: Google this sometime).

*

Margaret is back in Vancouver for her final meeting with the real estate people and suggested we meet up. I didn't invite Malcolm. I think she wanted me to be the intermediary.

Elizabeth's house (Margaret still called it her mother's house, which said something) has been sold to an organisation who develop sites. She didn't know the details – that was all left to the agent – and she didn't want to know. It was shedding something that was a bit of a concern. She was now unconcerned.

It had been advertised as a family home in need of renovation, with the potential for application to redevelop the plot. This let someone else decide: Retain a past or strike out for a future. It will be up to them. It could have gone to flesh-and-blood people but in the end it went to dollar-and-cent financiers.

She told me this in a pleasant but matter-of-fact way. She wasn't looking for any reaction.

I brought the conversation back round to Elizabeth and the research I had been doing.

 'So that was around 1972, Margaret, …..'

Visibly the penny dropped.

The man in her bed, the secrecy of her mother, the reason the man could not simply be turned out onto the street.

All history. All now slightly irrelevant. A past.

She took long slow sips of her coffee. Her face changed a few times. She was both processing what I had said but also calculating her response.

Eventually, she looked across at me and reeled off several jobs that she needed to do before flying out, and that she had better get going.

She did give me a smile and a relaxed, if perfunctory, hug as she left. She said that she would email me when she was settled back home.

*

If I don't become a best-selling writer, that might be a relief.

It would save me any Imposter Syndrome; worrying if my award-winning first novel is all I've got. Would I want the strain of having to produce a second novel that isn't a disappointment?

And if I became set in a style that works, churning out success after success, would I simply end up trapped in a closed world of the same characters acting in the same ways in the same settings?

And if I did then try to do something new, there would be uproar from my extensive and loyal fanbase – people whose purchases support me in what I do, but who expect too much, who think they know me better than I know myself.

Am I a writer? That reminds me of a poem by someone (Holub something, or something Holub?) essentially asking if the writer was a poet – and concluding that they had written poems (So used to be a poet) and intended to write poetry in the future (So would be a poet sometime). A poet is only a poet when actively writing poetry. A writer is only a writer when actively writing.

I am writing every day – some days more than others – so, yes, I am a writer.

How successful remains to be seen.

*

Earlier, I slipped a note under Malcolm's door. It seemed the appropriate thing to do. I had laid all of Elizabeth's stuff out for him to see. I had her story, pieced together, or as much as I could tell, with all its flaws and errors, ready for him to hear.

If he wanted to know what I knew, I was ready.

He was there in a flash. I didn't know he could move that quickly.

On the trestle table, objects were set out in a long line, ready for inspection. They were being paraded. No, more than that, her life was being laid out ready for dissection; ready for a post-mortem, an autopsy.

'This won't bring her back to life, but it might help bring her life back,' I said.

It sounded profound at the time. It seems pretentious after the event.

I took him along the line, one cluster of objects at a time, telling him the story that each had passed on to me.

Certificates:

Her parents and her. Born somewhere unpronounceable in Poland. Elzbieta, daughter of Agnieska and Josef.

Documents:

Entry to Germany for work and a home; then Bolton and onward to Vancouver.

Handmade doll:

Two young girls' love and promises sewn into this one of a pair; separated in Germany and later reunited, after two separate journeys, by two teenage girls in Vancouver who remained friends and neighbours.

Baby boots and cape:

More to be done to see what their story is. We may never know.

Letters and photographs:

Agnes and Elizabeth, so geographically close, so emotionally tied, yet so far apart. The death of her rather grumpy father not long after getting to the promised place. Elizabeth and friends in an artist/hippie encampment/colony, somewhere near the water. A happy trip to Seattle, buying a silk scarf. A morose man by a cabin. Others smiling in all seasons. A marriage to a man called Benjamin, who died. A daughter.

Photocopied pages from her Notebook:

Her domestic and personal jottings. Her thoughts. Her collected quotes and sketches. Her memories of individuals from those early days who had gone on to be artists, leaving her behind. These people doing half-forgotten exhibitions in small galleries.

People tying in with lost histories of the city. I asked Malcolm if he was aware of the 1930s occupations of buildings by the unemployed, the closure of library reading room, men being put to work on construction jobs, baton-wielding police clearing the various Jungle camps. He looked blank. 'All before my time,' he muttered.

Art catalogues, magazines and newspaper cuttings:

Elizabeth being a domestic who still hoped to be an artist. Her attempts to stay in touch, to wait in line – part-time courses, summer schools, outreach programmes: all in hope if not in reality. Frustrated aspirations building up the pressure until she found some release in Malcolm's offer of an apartment studio and some equipment.

Malcolm visibly swelled at that.

The formal letters:

She was a woman careful with money, doing her best, looking after everyone at some cost to herself. Taking any job as it came along, keeping things in good repair.

Library notes:

The draft dodging history of Vancouver, in which Elizabeth surely played her part even if it meant a court appearance and had cost her relationship with Margaret.

The nature of the West End, with all its richness, its seediness, its popularity and its changes.

The jewellery box:

Things hiding in plain sight. People not seeing what is plainly there for all to see. Things, and people, being overlooked.

I tried to give a sense of hidden histories being revealed as layer upon layer, all acted out against a shifting backdrop of an ever-changing Vancouver.

Malcolm listened in silence as I told the story.

I said that there were things he might add from his own understanding of Elizabeth, and that the neighbours from the funeral could add even more.

I told him that it was his responsibility now.

They were his things, his choice. Her legacy, but his to treat one way or another.

He could throw it all away. Elizabeth had given him permission to do that.

He could store it in a cupboard and bring it out from time to time, in remembrance.

Everything could be bundled up and sent over to the city Archive.

Or he could scatter bits here and there. I would take some. Margaret might want some.

I didn't tell him about the bit I had deliberately held back: The typed letter asking if the baby could be the unknown writer's. I didn't know who that belonged to.

Having brought her life together here on this mortuary trestle, it could be dismembered, fragmented and lost.

Malcolm looked up and down the length of objects on the table, then looked me up and down with the same expression.

'Well. You have done brilliantly. I never expected this much.'

'Glad you like it,' said rather more pointedly than I had intended. 'Maybe now I can get on with my life. Maybe now she will let me head back to New York.'

Malcolm leant over and rested an arm on my shoulder.

'Thankyou. Thankyou. This all comes at just the right time,' he said.

I'm not sure what he meant but I felt that he, too, was holding something back.

*

Two stories side by side in the newspaper today. Both with different takes on law, history, rights and reputations:

Justice Matthew Begbie. First judge of the Colony.1858. Gold Rush days. Impartially sorting out lawless miners across the Province for thirty-six years. He became fluent in some First Nation languages, sided with aboriginal land disputes and opposed settlers who wanted to squeeze people off their rightful lands. First Nation bands regarded him as a Big Chief.

When five First Nation leaders, defending their land, killed twenty people he could find no grounds for a reprieve so had to impose the mandatory death penalty for any murder of anyone, by anyone. The Chiefs were sentenced to be hanged.

A couple of years ago the Premier of British Columbia declared the chiefs to be fully exonerated of any crime. The Law Society of BC now want the judge's statue removed from their lobby. The once respected, native-friendly, miner-controlling, royally-knighted judge is now to be remembered as The

Hanging Judge. The Mighty fallen. The Hero as Villain – all for applying the law as it stood at the time. History judged by Now.

A historical fact being retold as some whole other story.

On the other page, a story of a long-standing dispute over a polygamy case coming to court. This has, apparently, been rumbling on for years, strung out on sets of legal niceties. What is in constitutional charters of rights and freedoms? What if no-one in that community objects?

Alternative versions, alternative facts, being bundled up around clear breaches of the law, including sex with minors, set against rights to religious freedoms. Justice Matthew Begbie would have it sorted in minutes, I think.

Come down on any side now and history will have an opinion.

*

BC election results: Two main parties separated by the closest of margins. All sides claiming victory (of course). Thousands of absentee votes still to be totted up, so people are still no nearer knowing who will finally be in control.

It seems that most elections are coming out 50/50. Maybe we have become, collectively, indecisive – splitting down the middle over most things.

Maybe, more than we care to admit it, life tends to come out 50/50; the toss of a coin; either/or; yes/no, with less and less room for subtleties and ambiguities. No, that's not it: Our lives are getting more and more ambiguous but the system (whatever that means) strives to put everything in binary.

It's either a 0 or it's a 1.

If you're not for it, you are against it. It is simply This, or it is That. Things can't stray across boxes when the computer gives only two choices.

Four of us (Malcolm, Margaret, Elizabeth and myself) have been doing a little dance around each other. How could we four split off 50/50?

Me and Malcolm; or Margaret and Elizabeth. Men or Women?

Me and Margaret; or Malcolm and Elizabeth. People with the potential to be friendly in the future, or People tied by old friendships rooted in the past?

Me and Elizabeth; or Margaret and Malcolm. People who are getting close, knowing the whole story, or People who have yet to work things out?

If it comes to it, if backs are against the wall, whose side would I want to be on?

More interestingly, at the end of everything, who would I want to have on my side?

*

It turns out that Malcolm has been a behind-the-scenes negotiator around the sale of Elizabeth's/Margaret's house.

As soon as I bumped into him he offered me a glass of red. I got the feeling that he was pleased with himself and had already had a couple. The story is that he has been talking to the finance organisation. They bought the land as part of their strategy to future-proof their funds based on rising land values. They will sell the land on to property developers but not for at least ten years. In the meanwhile, the organisation's charitable foundation will lease the house to Malcolm in the name of his rental company.

He will live there at no cost for so long as he acts as caretaker-curator of the home and its artworks. The house will hold Elizabeth's paintings – shown in the place where she lived out her little dramas. It will shift from being a home to being a place of memories. Not a memorial, not a mausoleum – just a place where people can sit and think, stimulated by the thoughts that Elizabeth captured in paint. It could be a springboard helping people move themselves forward, not a heritage-museum dragging people back to how things once were.

The place will be a base to research the reputation of Elizabeth as an artist.

The Foundation agreement allows for one-year part-time placements. There have been various interests already. A university researcher is tying it in with her work on women like Elizabeth as people who shaped Vancouver from below. Someone else is looking at what this art colony was, in so far as it really existed as something more than a few hippy dropouts squatting by the beach. Another researcher is working on the lifestyles of post-war Polish families in Vancouver.

It is not about getting ever more rarefied detail of the life of one woman, boring deeper and deeper into her private affairs. It will use Elizabeth (person and paintings) as a way to look sideward, to get other perspectives on things. It is a way of Elizabeth still making a contribution to think about the life of Vancouver.

Malcolm has written to the few people he knows in artworld circles, and they are contacting others.

The coffee-sipping neighbour is typing up what she remembers about Elizabeth, Agnes and her gruff husband.

Malcolm is to do some liaison work with various galleries around the province – particularly the smaller, less well-known ones. There will be programmes of public engagement activities.

The aim is to go outwards, to gather fragments and see what story they tell nowadays.

He will host open days, organise meetings, invite speakers.

I can imagine him as host, offering afternoon teas and glasses of wine.

He wouldn't be entitled to any salary but gets a home to live in, gets a role in life and, most importantly to him, gets to try to do best by Elizabeth's memory and standing.

He was full of it.

*

Days have gone past. I have sat in the library; listened to talks, been to the Museum, read the papers, drunk coffee, sifted through an old woman's few remaining treasures, and exchanged notes and emails.

In between I have been doing what, at its simplest, has been meagre people-watching.

I have my places. My hides. Spots at which I can sit and be invisible to those in my gaze. I am in full view, in plain sight, but no-one seems to notice me.

Starbucks, library, transit buses; the SkyTrain out to the airport. A few well-selected streets: Granville down from Robson; East Hastings three blocks from the steam clock; the length of Denman.

I sit, stare and make jottings.

I capture street scenes. Snapshots in words: framed, composed, toned and coloured.

These are my take on the world. They are snippets. They are my abstractions. fragments of a whole.

They are impressions fixed, out of place, out of time, out of context: producing something no longer factually real.

I love watching people.

Jane Jacobs put it well: Eyes on the street, people being out and about; a daily ballet of people dancing themselves through their daily routines.

People's lives shaped by the spaces around them.

Grids may look neat on paper. Those New York city planners may have been right, and drivers need to be able to move around. Jane Jacobs may have been more right, in that it is about humanity sharing a public space.

Cities are our backdrop. Cities with their nooks and crannies, their gaps between buildings. Allowing us to peer round corners, exploring, with a sense of adventure and mystery – peeking into places where we catch glimpses of our own lives as fleeting shadows, here and there, seen out of the corner of our eye.

*

Margaret emailed as she said. Just a short one, hoping I was well. No mention of our conversation. Inviting a reply, none-the-less.

I didn't want to dwell on the house, or on her mother, so I asked what job she had done in finance, saying that I didn't really understand the world of economics. She banged a reply straight back. I think she wants me as a friend, or a pen-pal or something. I'm not sure what I think about that. It seemed churlish not to reply but I don't really want an extended conversation with her.

Don,

I was a financial forensic analyst. I was employed by a prestigious financial firm but mostly was a hired hand, sold to other agencies to help with financial puzzles like tracking the routes taken by missing millions from various countries. I kept an eye on ill-gotten gains of autocrats and plutocrats across the globe. Sometimes this was on behalf of Federal agencies here. Sometimes it was on a contract internationally. If you like, I kept oversight of various large ledgers. It was nothing more than that. It was a bit of extended bureaucracy.

You may think it sounds fascinating. At one level it was. At another level it was just routine computer number-crunching. The skill was, I suppose, in interpreting what the numbers were trying to tell us. Or, rather, what the numbers were trying to hide from us.

When we met for coffee, you said that you could never be an economist. People think that economics is some weird and complicated thing, a view sustained by most economists. Really it can be very simple.

From one perspective life is one huge Ponzi scheme. Bits of money are endlessly taken from lots of people in lots of ways, mostly involving some form of deception, and fed upwards to a few at the top of the pyramid who live as if there will always be an endless supply of cash coming to them.

Everyday life is full of simple deceptions. People choose one breakfast cereal over another, thinking they have a favourite brand. Both brands are, however, put out by the same food company, which in turn is part of some larger conglomerate, which is kept going by investors shoring it up for as long as the excess cash keeps being pumped up to them. Society is a simple money machine whereby the rich get richer at the expense of those many poorer people who, even if they don't get any poorer, certainly don't get much richer in real terms.

For most people, life is simply not having enough money to be able to change their lives. They hold out for having enough to get by on, plus maybe the chance to own some property that might get handed on to children in the hope that this will give the kids a better start in life. For them the problem is never quite having enough money.

It is for them that I got into economics in the first place.

Margaret

I sent a brief response and got something far more personal in response. I imagined her alone in her Toronto home with a glass of red wine:

Don,

The Job is left far behind. I don't expect calls from ex-colleagues inviting me to drinks or for meals. We never had those sort of relationships, at the best of times. I was a manager amongst managers.

My childhood, tied into that house, also feels gone now that the house is sold. Of course, I have strong memories of Mother, and have had to rearrange those a bit now that I know about those other sides of her.

The apartment in Toronto has never felt like a home. It has always been simply a place to live, an asset. I could move out tomorrow. I could travel. I could go anywhere.

I have banked the money from the transfer of the house. I am OK with that. I have always found money and balance sheets easier to deal with than real things like house repairs (or people).

My own balance looks a great deal healthier. It isn't about money though. At the end of the day it is about what you want to do with money.

At nights, I can drift into thinking of this money as my own ill-gotten gain. It has been tracked to me. I am the guilty party.

So now what do I do? At the selfish level, one chunk pays off my apartment off leaving me with more than enough pension income to live on. At the public-good level, one chunk will set up a fund to support young artists, particularly at-risk young people. It seems fitting, even if there is the tinge of it being some sort of penance.

Love

Margaret

*

What happens to Elizabeth's few treasures now that Malcolm has his grand plan for her?

The paintings are his to own, to display, and eventually – if his plan doesn't work out - to sell or destroy. The house remains standing for as long as Malcolm can get people using it. If that doesn't work out, the Foundation cash in their asset and move on.

The letters are personal to Margaret but aren't owned by her. Elizabeth deliberately put things beyond Margaret's reach. I'm not sure that is necessary now. Margaret seems a lovely person who does the right things in life – but it seemed the right decision to Elizabeth at the time. I'm sure Elizabeth wouldn't want them on public display.

The other things: The scarf, the doll, documents, some of her notebooks – all can be the beginnings of Malcolm setting Elizabeth's life out for all to react to.

*

Observing homeless street people:

1. A man slumped on the sidewalk outside Tim Hortons; half with-it, half out of it; cigarette dangling aimlessly. Wearing a leather coat that would look trendy on anyone else but which, on closer inspection, turned out to be

frayed and caked. Boots: His boots are sensible workman's boots. When the factories collapsed back home he lost his job but kept his boots. Hair greying, poking out under a hood that covers much of his face – not wanting to show his pain to the world – age indecipherable. Empty coffee cup in an outstretched hand.

2. Another man, in an outfit that doesn't feel appropriate. Forage cap, combat jacket and pants. Army boots. Some street commando geared up for battles the day will throw at him. Wanting the chaos of his life to be regimented by someone, anyone. Longing to be part of a squad. His face is unnaturally pale, twitching.

3. A woman curled in on herself as best she can. Mumbling. Plastic sheet pulled tight round herself, and beneath that, under layers and layers, somewhere there is an emaciated body. A somebody who is a nobody. From her wrist is a length of string tied to a cart piled with plastic bags. Her accumulated treasures.

From that report on homelessness, there are more than three thousand more like these. The fastest growth is out in the suburbs not in the central city district, which surprises me. Even the homeless get pushed outwards (out to the fringes, the margins, even more on edge) as hostels get turned into smart apartments for creative incomers.

Could I ever be one of them (homeless person, not a creative incomer)? For many, it is just a couple of steps away: a family argument; a bout of real depression; the loss of a couple of months pay; an accumulating debt…..

For now, I stand a couple of steps away from them as I wait in line for my coffee and they wait on the pavement outside.

Others, on the inside:

1. She looks Irish, yet I don't even know what I mean when I say that. She has the look of a gypsy girl? She has tousled raven hair? Her dark eyes have a longing in them? Caricatures, all of it.
    She looks up. I look away. I could have smiled but it didn't seem right. How can it not feel right to smile at someone?
    She looks back at her magazine. I stare at her bent head.
    She's just a regular young woman. She could be anyone; could be anything. So why does she make all these impressions of gypsy Irish abandon stick to her? What makes her appear to be some sort of vulnerable runaway; a slightly lost soul?

2. An older guy. Glasses and beard. If I said 1970s liberal studies professor, that would immediately give the picture. That would have him pinned.
Creases from smiling too much. Laughter lines. Love lines. Casual dress. Casual guy. He spends his time people watching. This is awkward: Me watching him, watching me, watching him

3. Young Mom. Striped knitted top, a bit baggy on her. Baby, unseen, grizzling in stroller. She stares distractedly at nothing in particular. A sign of medium to severe sleep deprivation. Her mind is blank. Anything could be written on it. It used to take Koreans several days to get captured American soldiers to this state. She looks as if she could collapse down onto her arms and sleep for hours.
She stays awake, alert to the baby, half-dead to anything else.
She looks like an affluent version of that person I saw first responders dealing with yesterday out on Granville – standing upright, leaning forward, rigidly comatose; in a zombie-like trance, frozen by the new drug sweeping the city.

4. Grey-haired woman. String of pearls. That seems to say so much about her.

Delicate earrings. Just a bit of lipstick. Simple pink top, black slacks, sensible shoes. Lines at the edges of her mouth – from too many expressions of distaste? Skin on her thin and wrinkled hands, crisscrossed with stand-out veins.

She looks bemused, as if life used not to be like this. As if there used to be a nice little place doing Kaffee und Kuchen, and a chance to speak the old language – and now time has relegated her to a coffee chain with doughnuts and the chance to be looked down on by graduates on temporary contracts.

I watch her, silently sipping coffee, away in her own thoughts, and I imagine a solitary life in a decent enough apartment somewhere nearby.

All this reminds me that the city is starting a conversation on loneliness. Beyond all the calmness and the politeness, there is sadness. These people could well be some of the thousands who rarely go out; who never talk to anyone.

This city may be one of the most liveable cities; may have packed sidewalks, but people are moving silently next to each other. It adds to the calmness, but maybe there are benefits in a bit of New York raucousness.

Maybe Vancouver would gain by being just a bit more snarly.

*

A note under my door, from Malcolm, thanking me for all my work in the difficult task of sorting through Elizabeth's belongings.

He wanted to tell me more about the plans.

The Centre ('centre' now, not just a house) is funded for three years, to give time to establish itself and find innovative ways of income generation.

Would I consider being a member of the Steering Group?

It will comprise no more than six people.

A Group of Six.

A group of seven would have seemed like fun to me; but Malcolm doesn't do fun.

Malcolm is one 'by right' (his term); Margaret has agreed to be another; the Foundation will want to nominate one to keep an eye on things for them; plus someone from the art environment or a university – and me.

We will meet twice a year. Return travel from anywhere in North America and two night's hotel accommodation paid for.

Malcolm will be our eyes and ears as it were. The man on the ground. I think in his mind that was capitalised: The Man on the Ground.

This will keep a tie between the three of us – Malcolm, Margaret and myself (Why in that order? Why do I always put myself last?).

The two of them, Malcolm and Margaret, (and Elizabeth in her own way), are now part of my history.

I won't easily shake them off.

*

The new rental agreement arrived for New York apartment. Next email was (predictably) Jerry up in arms.

*

My time is up. I have five days to sign up to the rental terms or find somewhere else.

I don't know what to do. My life has a jaggedness to it. There is an uneasiness – that's the best I can do at the moment.

It is not a matter of deciding where I want to be. It is more about deciding what I want to be; or how I want to be.

So, what are the choices:

New York or Vancouver?

USA or Canada?

Arrogance or Simplicity?

Clamour or Courtesies?

Trump or Trudeau?

Standing Out or Fitting In?

Star Spangled Banner or O Canada?

Fake News or No News?

Writing or Something Else?

Doing or Being?

Staying Me or Becoming Someone Else?

That is a good enough list to base a choice on.

Score on a scale of 1 to 10. Add up each side. Act on that.

Criteria-based decision-making.

What else is there? Gut Feeling? Throwing a dice?

Of course, it doesn't have to be starkly here or there; this or that.

There are other places – Toronto, Edmonton, Winnipeg, Seattle, Portland, but wherever I go, it will definitely be a city, so there are still likely to be the same issues:

gentrification; unaffordable housing; changing demographics; health/poverty issues; waterfront renovations

homelessness; helplessness; coalitions and collusions; death on the street; just-managing struggling families

sceneries and viewpoints; water and woodland; bobbing boats and full ferries; iconic buildings and public memorials; creatives and entrepreneurs.

Most of all, wherever I end up, there will be people with hopes and dreams, people wanting something better.

People like Elizabeth.

People like me.

Whatever I do, it will include writing of some sort. I want to stay true to Grandad Donald. I want to be aware of the potential around me.

However I live, it is likely to be more definite, more determined, more interesting

– more like Elizabeth in many ways.

I am heading out for a coffee, to settle my future, and to get words on paper.

A Life in Fragments

(first 2000 words of my planned novel)

I have walked these same streets for the last twenty years. I have sat and stared. I have watched and watched. I am familiar with every building. I am intimate with every vacant lot.

I watch the city change. I see all the likely futures – films unspooling in my head – each possibility becoming more or less likely as the day settles itself on the city.

Over the years I have progressively become the city and the city has become me. Undivided. Indivisible.

I sense things that others don't. I'm not talking about ghosts and stuff, just feelings as the city tells me things.

I used to think that everyone did that. Maybe it's just me. Maybe it's my little quirk.

I wouldn't know. I don't talk much to other people.

My mother always said that I was a strange child, sitting alone at the bottom of the stairs, staring at my foot, lost in thought, saying nothing.

I saw a film once, about a tornado. Everything was being sucked up into it, spun around faster and faster, then thrown out.

'That's my brain, there.'

'You say the strangest things, Lizzie. You really do.'

I didn't say much after that.

She used to ask what I was thinking. I wouldn't tell her what was in my head. I couldn't tell her anything. It was none of her business. It was better that she didn't know.

When things spun too fast, that's when I had to stare at one point and let some bit of me become all there was in the world. If I didn't then I would start to fly off in all directions.

I would disintegrate.

Especially on Wednesdays.

Wednesdays had a vague feeling to them that clouded everything, like a thin mist, stopping me finding the point I needed to fix on, letting bits of me stream off into the world.

I had to shut my eyes and stay perfectly still until things stopped spinning.

I didn't do much on Wednesdays.

Mom would tell the school that I was having one of my usual Wednesday migraines. I got to stay home.

We went to the hospital once, but they didn't find anything.

It was on a Tuesday.

Anyway, she died.

That was a year after I started work.

A woman from the housing association came and got her taken away.

I hadn't known what to do, so I phoned them.

The woman came back the next day and said that I would have to move out.

I started to sleep in the park.

Mom dying was sad.

Leaving the apartment to live in the park was hard. I cried. A lot.

That was when I was young.

I have it all under control now.

Things are stopped down good and proper.

I am in charge. No bits streaming off me.

Just normal.

It's by walking the same route, over and over, that things stay controlled.

It is by walking the streets that I notice each tiny change.

I sense where the city is starting to wear thin. This is where history leaks through.

I don't see anything.

I feel it. I sense it.

History is there. It knows that I am here, and it reaches through to make itself known.

Old signs leak through the boarding and plaster that cover them.

Buried things make themselves known.

Even dead bodies.

I know that they lie there, unseen, because of the way my brain works.

The doctor talked about wiring, but I don't think there is wiring in my brain.

It feels like something alive - flows, and tentacles – not mechanical things like wirings.

Put people like me into one of their scanners and they won't see wirings. They will see colours and patterns.

I draw a lot. Pencil drawings on paper I get from the printshop on the corner. Offprints, they call it.

Something they don't want. Paper, I call it.
Somewhere to sketch what is in my brain.

Mostly what's in there are patterns, zigzags, arcs and
perspectives: all the comings and goings of the city.

I put it on paper to get it out of my head.

I draw it from memory. Some people think I have
these little pictures in my head and I copy them out
onto the offprint papers. It's not like that at all. Bits
come together and its only when the fragments
overlap that everything forms a pattern and makes
some sort of sense.

I like Detective Kowalski. He is one of the good cops.

He says that's because he never worked Vice or
Drugs, stuck to Homicide and never let himself get
leant on. He says that once a cop gets leant on and
bends, they have to bend further and further until they
end up broken.

I've known him all my life.

If I was wandering alone in the street, he would take
me home to Mom. He never made a big deal of it, just
said that I shouldn't be wandering about on my own,
and that he needed some company so would I walk
with him as far as my house. Mom always thanked
him, I remember that.

He was here, walking the beat, well before the area changed over to all beardy-types and craft beer.

When I left school, and worked in the factory down the road, he still looked out for me.

'You're a regular girl with a regular job now,' he used to say to me. He still walked home with me and still spent a few minutes checking on Mom and how she was getting along.

He was the one who introduced me to the police psychologist.

That was after Mom died and after I moved out of the apartment.

There were times when people came to find me. They tried to get me to live in an apartment. I tried it for a while but then they started talking about arrears, and responsibilities, and I moved back to the park.

Kowalski used to call on me every day and one time said that there was someone who wanted to meet me. He said that she worked with him and that I could trust her.

It turned out she was interested in how I thought about things.

She told me I had an asset. I didn't know what an asset was, but I was pleased that I had one. She asked me what went on in my head as I walked around an area.

I told her about hot feelings and cold feelings. About hot spots and cold spots. She said it might help them investigate.

I didn't know how that fitted in with what the police did. We had a deal. I didn't want to know, and they didn't want me to be part of their investigation team.

I was willing to wander around. I was willing to tell the psychologist about any feelings. That was enough for me.

She came to the factory some days. The boss let me go early. Or she came to the park. She always knew where to find me and never pushed me to get back in an apartment.

She took me for walks around bits of the city I hadn't been to before. I told her what I felt.

In return, the psychologist fixed me up with hot meals in their canteen, gave me coffees and pastries to go, and hugged me gently. I liked the hugs.

One time, when a little girl went missing, she took me over to a wooded area. She said that the police had reason to believe this was an area of interest.

We had to scramble well off the path, through an area full of brambles, to a bit of a clearing. If anything was of interest back there it was well away from prying eyes.

I walked round and round. There were no feelings of anything but raw earth. There was no disturbed soil. The sniffer dog the police had brought wandered round disinterested.

'Nothing,' we all agreed. 'False lead.'

Detective Kowalski seemed disappointed but didn't let it show much.

'Sorry folks. It was always an off-chance, but it is all we have for now.'

He walked off. The police dog was led away. The psychologist was left looking round the small clearing.

I ducked under an old tree branch, ready to head off round the bramble patches, when there was this sudden surge in my left leg.

The psychologist was about to call everyone back, but I told her that the feeling was of something old not a young thing, and something manufactured not some living (or dead) body. She called people back anyway.

The policeman with the shovel only had to scrape off a top layer of soil, right above where the surge had been strongest, before he struck something.

He lifted it out and dusted off the loose soil.

It was wooden. A box: too small to be called a trunk; too large to be called a jewellery box. A casket I would have said.

The police took it back to the lab to have a good look at it. The medical examiner opened it in a screened cupboard.

'No toxic mould,' he said, 'and any dangerous dust has been sucked right away by now. There is only paper in there, so far as I can see. It's safe to inspect it, so long as you wear rubber gloves and keep it under a plastic sheet.'

No-one had asked me to leave, so I stayed. Something was telling me that I needed to be there.

Kowalski took the stuff out of the casket and laid things along a bench. He talked to himself.

'Some letters. All handwritten. Nothing typed. They might look old but they are on modern paper, the sort you buy at any stationery store.

This one talks of Last Will and Testament. Can't make out the name properly but looks like Ernest Gottlieb or Gottfried.

This next is some sort of land-claim document. In Spanish. It mentions Bolivia.

This here is a map of old New York, There are circles dotted around, out by the water's edge. Lower East Side; Battery; out near Pier 46; and others in the tangle of streets bordering on Chinatown. Nothing on any of the main grid routes. The circles make some sort of pattern, but nothing regular. A constellation of points, but nothing recognizable. The map looks to be around the early 1900s.'

He looked up.

'That's all folks. No idea what any of it refers to. It doesn't connect to our missing-girl case, so it will all go in the store until we decide what to do with it. Note it down as Lost and Found: see if anyone claims it. Unlikely, I think.'

Somebody had carefully put those few papers in there and shallow-buried it out of the way in a hard-to-visit wooded area.

I had an overwhelming sense of needing to know about the person who had owned that casket.

Who were you?

Why did you do that?

I had to find out.

I had to piece it all together.

That's when my life changed.

***

That was the past and, for me, only that past was real. Everything since then has felt a bit like me being caught up in a fiction created by the owner of that casket. That was twenty years ago. A lot has happened since then.

38208552R00115

Printed in Poland
by Amazon Fulfillment
Poland Sp. z o.o., Wrocław